Nod Ghosh lives in Christchurch, New Zealand and graduated from the Hagley Writers' Institute in 2012.

Nod's short fiction has been widely published internationally and placed in competitions including the Bath Flash Fiction Award.

Truth Serum Press has published three books featuring novellae-in-flash: *The Crazed Wind* (2018), *Filthy Sucre* (2020) and *Toy Train* (2021).

Two novellas are due for publication in 2023: *Throw A Seven* by *Reflex Press* and *The Two-Tailed Snake,* by *Fairlight Books.*

Nod works as a medical laboratory scientist in Christchurch, diagnosing leukaemia and lymphoma, and is a relief teacher for *Write On, School for Young Writers.*

Find more at http://www.nodghosh.com/about/

LOVE, LEMONS AND ILLICIT *SEX*

NOD GHOSH

TRUTH SERUM PRESS

Truth Serum Press
32 Meredith Street
Sefton Park SA 5083
Australia

Email: truthserumpress@live.com.au
Website: truthserumpress.net
Catalogue: truthserumpress.net/catalogue

Cover image copyright © Nod Ghosh
Cover design copyright © Matt Potter
Author photograph copyright © Heather Matthews, used with permission

Also available as an ePub eBook
ISBN: 978-1-923000-09-4
Also available as a Kindle eBook
ISBN: 978-1-923000-12-4

Truth Serum Press is a member of the
Bequem Publishing collective
bequempublishing.com

Dedicated to those who like
Madeleine, Zeb and John XY
yielded to temptation.

Errare humanum est – to err is human.
To persevere – entirely understandable.

Contents

Making the Words
Fit the Story

It's not easy, but I lock eyes with the boy. The cafeteria is almost empty.

"It's you I'm concerned about," I say.

I feel vulnerable, even though I'm the adult here.

He's hardly spoken. When he speaks, he doesn't follow the script.

"You want to do it again, don't you?"

"No," I sit back. "There's a reason it's illegal."

A seafront cliff – ninety percent darkness – his skin – the roaring waves.

"You're worried I'll tell," he says.

Of course I'm worried.

"That's not why I'm concerned." I fix my eyes on his. "I need to know if you were harmed when – when – "

"When we fucked?"

After a week of incriminating texts, I've agreed to meet him here.

"Do you need anything? Only – you mustn't tell anyone." I hate the quaver of my voice.

His hand creeps up my thigh. My words trail off.

Twenty minutes later, we're in my bed doing it again.

Unlike the hesitant boy from the beach, his strokes are confident, urgent.

I've known him since he was nine, a slight, quiet child.

Whenever he stayed over, he'd wash his dish after breakfast. My son's other friends left theirs. But this boy was tidy, methodical.

I liked his mother too. We did things together. Climbing the Port Hills. Concerts. Camping with the children. We stayed friends after they'd drifted apart. You see that with boys; their friendships change when their voices do.

After my divorce, I was lonely. The boy's mother helped, knew what to say, and what not to, because she'd been through it. Her child was a baby when his father's eye had wandered. We became closer; saw each other every week, watched our sons grow up.

The ex took my boy overseas for a month when he turned sixteen.

I called her because I was lonely.

"We're going to Taylor's," she said. "Why don't you join us? We have space."

"Oh, I couldn't intrude."

"You must."

So I shared the lazy end of summer with them, a time when the lonely can self-destruct without company.

We played cards, laughed a lot. She poured wine into our glasses, didn't stop him filling his own. He put some ethereal music on the sound system. The notes worked their fingers over my body.

"What *is* this?" I turned up the volume. 'It's so − so captivating. Sensual."

"It's mine," the boy said. "I made it."

"Oh."

He was growing up so fast.

The mother slipped out into the black-green dark. I poured more wine. He thrashed me at gin rummy.

Later, I ventured out to find her. The sand was warm on my bare feet.

Footsteps crunched behind me. I turned expecting to see her.

Instead, I saw her son's lean body backlit by yellow light.

"I can't find your mum."

"She's asleep." His voice cracked. "Let's walk."

The surf's roar silenced our words. We climbed up beyond the beach huts.

At the plateau, we pushed through grass towards a bench that faced the ocean. Waves crashed. If we wandered too far, we'd fall to our deaths on the rocks below.

~

I don't remember who made the first move. It doesn't matter, because I should have stopped it. Instead, I kissed him. My hands went to places they shouldn't.

He wasn't hard and that frightened me, brought home the reality of the situation: he was a *child*.

"Are you okay?" I hesitated. The ocean roared like a train.

"Yes." His breathing was heavy. He guided me. "Do it like this."

I pulled back.

"How old are you now, anyway?"

"Eighteen."

I swallowed his lie with our kiss.

The next morning, his mother was subdued.

I asked where he was.

"Asleep," she said. "Do you have aspirin?"

In my room, I shook the sand from my dirty clothes.

Dirty.

I couldn't stay.

I took her some paracetamol.

"It's all I have."

She dry swallowed them.

"Hey. Something's come up," I said. "I need to go."

She didn't ask why. Didn't offer to help.

~

In the weeks that followed, I didn't contact her.

I saw him when the kids went back to school.

My boy nodded at his old friend, ran to a group of newer ones. The boy leaned against a post, staring as I drove away.

I attempted a smile.

I rang his mother.

"Did I do something to offend you?" she asked.

"What? No. Why?"

"You left that day. Didn't say a word."

"I –"

"Then I don't hear from you for a month."

"I've been, you know." I couldn't think what I'd been.

I offered to take her out for dinner, asked if she'd seen there was a new play on at the Adelphi. Perhaps we could go together?

She said she was too busy.

His text arrived that night.

– *Why have you been staying away?*

I didn't reply.

An hour later:

– *Haven't heard back. I'm coming round.*

– *Don't come,* I messaged. *I won't be in.*

– *You are. I can see you.*

I pulled the curtains tighter, peered through a crack, saw no one there.

He rang the next day, but I didn't answer.

He texted that night. Words of a desperate boy. Perhaps he believed he was in love. Maybe part of me wanted him to be.

I replied, urged him to mix with girls his own age.

– *What would you have done?* he asked. *Would you have gone to the police?*

– *What do you want?*

– *I think we should meet.*

So that's what we did.

Now he's in my bed, hungry, forceful.

It was never like this with my husband.

It was never this good.

And then … there's glass in his eyes.

I lean over to kiss him, but he turns away.

"Are you all right?" I ask.

"No." He rolls out of bed. "The question is, are *you* all right?"

He slams the door and I'm left aching.

Seven Lesbians
and a Bar of Soap

I've had seven so far. Maybe more. China plinks ice into my overfull glass. The volume of liquid suggests the number is irrelevant.

I've had too much to drink, and it's long past midnight.

Red light on her cheeks, bones like porcelain, China's African dance tunes beat the air like molten syrup. She closes the sliding doors on June night light, dark as pencil lead.

Leilani pecks China on the cheek, proprietorial. Leilani's hair is streaked with bottled sun. China's is as black as swans. I want to touch it with my lips until it squeaks.

Sugar lights a cigarette and dances to a tune in her head.

Sugar sweet *petit fours* and Pavlova topped with kiwifruit line up for attention on china dessert plates. I sip my gin and tonic; the bitter bite of quinine no stranger to my palate.

I want more.

China pours me another. The thump-thump-thump of blood somewhere near my middle ear warns me to stop.

Lines of lemon decorate the starboard side of the cocktail bar. She squeezes citrus into the blackness of my glass.

"For you."

"Sweet as," I say, and she slips a slice of green fruit studded with seeds into my mouth.

Leilani pulls China away, her fingers laced through her lover's. She tugs her towards the light, away from me.

"I forgot the starter," she says. "Give me a hand." With graceless moves, Leilani assembles ceviche. Knife on board. Chop. Her finger oozes blood, telltale streaks of red on white flesh. Fennel fronds and coriander sprinkled like rags over the fish.

Fait accompli. Bon appétit.

But it's too late. Leilani is too late.

Fait accompli.

Teri's netball-toned leg protrudes from a dog-brown blanket on the sofa.

"Where's Helen?" she asks, her waking voice is treacle thick. She waves away the dish Leilani offers.

Maxine and Sugar refuse the fish too. Their teeth skitter like tambourines. A smattering of dust under noses tells a story they're not ready to share.

The ceviche is untouched.

It's definitely too late.

Sugar changes the music. The singer's dusty tones match the frisson of *want* in the air. Does Sugar *know* what's happening? She dances with Maxine's head on her shoulder. They rotate like twin engines.

"Did anyone see Helen?" Teri asks again, delirious with sleep. A line of women, shoes on, shoes off, locate the buzz from the bedroom, like rats in a Skinner box.

The hum of Helen's *Lelo* crescendoes in ursine waves. Her cries sound like fur between teeth.

"Who's she with?" Teri growls. Leilani checks for China's presence, accounted for by virtue of a hand in hers. We count the line of women with our eyes. We count ourselves. Teri, Leilani, China, Sugar, Maxine and me.

"She's on her own," Maxine smiles, her teeth white against her skin. We tiptoe away.

"Hey! The spa-pool! Let's go in." Teri's bright demeanor brought on to mask her embarrassment. En route, we drop clothes, black, red and party-white, discarded like spent weapons. We jump into the pool, watch its level rise. The cycle of lights, yellow, lime, emerald, cornflower, violet, red like disaster, orange, kōwhai yellow and back to the colour of fruit China pushed into my mouth.

Helen appears, her face oval with satisfaction. She slops into the pool.

China wears designer lingerie, like she knew this was going to happen. I stare at the delicate ridge of her collarbone and hope the transparency of my desire is smothered by splashes and inattention. The jets roar into action and a head of foam builds like packaging against the sides of the tub. It accumulates between seven bodies, glistening like fish, cubes of fish in a box. It expands until there is no watery meniscus. The cold kiss of night air makes no impact on warm bodies.

The foam grows.

"Did someone put soap in here?" Leilani hisses. "Turn the jets off." A wall of froth threatens to suffocate us. Sugar's fingers slip on the controls. The lights are extinguished. A rabbit's tail of suds climbs towards my nose. I think China winks at me through tufts of foam, though it's hard to tell in the dark.

There's a splash. Leilani screams. And in the tangle of limbs that ensues, the serpentine curl of fingers in mine assures me I have not imagined tonight.

China's eyes lock on mine as she squeezes my hand.

And the foam climbs, until it tips out in ermine waves.

The Carpet

It was the devil that made me do it.

Chris's folks, Faith and Vince, call every year. I make out I'm as broken as they are about their daughter's disappearance. She's been gone nineteen years, but Faith says it feels like yesterday. Eleanor hovers nearby, but I turn away so she can't hear my empty platitudes. I don't want my wife to think I'm still sweet on my old girlfriend.

Faith's voice chokes up.

"Do you think we'll ever find her, Manny?" She sounds like her daughter. Whining. Simpering. "Vince and I are going to Morocco again in March."

And that devil makes me say, "You've got to try, Faith. You've got to try."

I don't think about Chris often. It's when I see that damn Moroccan carpet though, I remember what I did. I should get rid of the fucking thing, but I can't. Not when I think what it's worth.

You can't throw out something that cost someone their life.

Chris and I started dating when we were sixteen. By the summer I turned eighteen I was ready for adventure. I needed to escape from the small town mentality eating me up, and threatening to spit me out onto the conveyer belt that led to meat and two veg, wife-and-a-mortgage. Babies. It's what she wanted, a ring on her finger, and a semi on the street where Faith and Vince lived.

It scared the crap out of me.

I wanted to travel. I wanted to explore realities that were different from my own. I wanted to feel the danger and excitement of alternative lifestyles.

Then everything changed, Chris's parents gave her a ton of money for her birthday. They wanted her to 'broaden her horizons' before she married and had kids.

"Go see the world," Vince said. They paid for me to travel with her, so she'd be safer. That kind of shames me now.

So instead of hitching round France on my own, I found myself with an Interrail ticket and a timid girlfriend tagging along. The trains across Europe made Chris travelsick. The rickety boat from Algeciras to Tangier was even worse, vomit swilling about on bathroom floors. Our adventure pretty much ended when we came ashore in the turgid Moroccan heat. She started throwing up within minutes of entering our hotel room.

Chris lay on the hotel bed like a mannequin. She stared at the beige paint peeling off the ceiling. Her hair splayed out on the pillow like wind-blown wheat. Her paper-white skin made her look like a corpse. I did what I felt I ought, a fly caught in a web, itching to break the strands of her sticky embrace.

I went to the market, bought fruit that Chris sunk in sterilising fluid and ate in little chunks. She ran to the toilet every hour.

"I'm sorry, Manny," she said.

"What for?" I asked, choking back the resentment. "You can't help being sick." I bubbled with anger and tried not to think about what I'd be doing if I weren't playing nursemaid.

By rights, I shouldn't have been with Chris anymore. But if I hadn't stuck it out, I'd have had to kiss Morocco goodbye. Go figure.

On the third day, Chris told me she was feeling better. Her skin had stopped burning. She even managed a meal of flat bread and kefta. I suggested we go out. We pulled djellabas from the market over our heads to blend in, so the hawkers wouldn't hassle us. It didn't help. I felt the hot breath of traders on my neck, offering gold, slippers, porcelain. Anything. Chris leaned on me and took little steps, like a spider heavy with eggs.

We turned left then right, right then left, ended up lost. Boys with menacing grins dashed about looking important. Hooded figures hunched over hookahs. Women with secret smiles, heads wrapped in coloured cloth.

We stopped at a bar and ordered beer for me, mint tea for her. Chris disappeared to the bathroom. I got chatting to a guy called Mustapha, my French broken and basic. Chris came back, smiled and nodded. Her French was worse than mine.

Mustapha offered to take us to places the average tourist didn't know about. Said he could show us *the real Morocco*. He spoke fast, over the twang of tuneless instruments. He talked about cheap carpets and jewellery in his uncle's shop. My French wasn't brilliant, but I thought he said something about getting some shit hot hash, too. The stuff I'd picked up at the souk was all right, but I wanted some black.

Mustapha whistled and a boy trotted over. He was about eight, wore a pair of holed shorts and a 'Manchester United' T-shirt. They spoke in Arabic. The kid ran off.

By the time the boy returned, it was dark outside. Mustapha led us to a battered turquoise taxi. We wound through narrow streets, all the time feeling like we were being sucked into the guts of a giant creature.

We stepped out of the car to face a tall narrow building. The hot air wrapped itself around me like a blanket. Chris walked slowly, like everything was a huge effort. We followed Mustapha into a building that had no shop frontage, no signs, no indication that we were entering anything but an ordinary apartment block. Chris looked back at me once, questioning, silent, as if checking how precarious our situation was, appealing for reas-surance. I forced a smile.

The uncle's carpet shop appeared to have opened just for us. A toothless man greeted us.

"Most welcoming. You for shopping come," he said, obsequious and foul. "Many, many goods we had. Come, come." He led us up narrow wooden steps, through a door with a faded sign on it: 'Tiger Carpets', with a cartoon animal, paint chipped, Arabic beneath the English letters.

One of the men urged Chris and I to sit on two low wooden stools. Two skinny guys brought out stacks of carpets. One of the guys was a midget. Mustapha stood in the corner looking as if he'd been given a reward, his teeth shining eggshell white in the light of a flickering bare light bulb.

"Many month to make," the toothless uncle lisped. He threw rugs about like he was dealing cards. "Childlen from stleet work loom. We feed. Like own son and daughter." A woman scuttled in with a tray holding a long-spouted pot and pastel coloured glass cups. She broke pieces of loafsugar into the cups, bowed and padded out again. One of Mustapha's uncles served steaming tea. Mustapha passed me a pipe, and I took a toke without question. Chris nodded it away, so I passed the metal pipe to the old feller. My head spun with a thousand coloured cobwebs.

Then *the carpet* appeared. I'd never seen anything like it. The size of a bath mat, but beautiful. Like the pattern on a dragonfly's wing, laced with peacock iridescence. I ran my finger through its deep pile, imagining a child working for months to make the intricate pattern. Blues and golds. Chris's eyes lit up. Her face glistened in the odd light.

Toothless asked how much money we had. Chris gave me a warning look, and I put my hand on her shoulder.

She was hot again. I offered forty Dirhams. He dismissed my offer like I'd slapped his face.

A hookah appeared. More tea. Photographs of grandchildren. The room was spinning by the time I parted with 370 Dirhams. It was half our budget for the week.

Toothless bundled our carpet into a brown bag along with a 'Tiger Carpets' card. The same goofy cartoon tiger we'd seen on the sign outside the door.

I slid the pack into my shoulder bag, and listened to the thumping of my heart within my chest. There was the promise of something exciting in the air. We'd blown a huge amount of cash, but I didn't care. We were on the gateway to something incredible, the real Morocco. Chris was shaking.

Mustapha offered to show us gold jewellery. I told him I didn't want that. I wanted to see *the real Morocco*. I wanted to get hold of whatever had been in that pipe. That was what I'd come for. That was how *my* horizons were going to be broadened. That was my gold. The men mumbled to each other, and indicated we should follow the short guy.

The midget spoke little French or English, but he said enough through gesticulation for us to know he would take us where we wanted to be.

"Go with him," Mustapha said with a smile.

"You not coming?" Chris asked.

"I have to work." He shrugged.

~

The little guy's drooping eyelids gave him a sleepy appearance. Chris and I followed the man out to an alley. We entered another tall narrow building. I followed two steps behind the midget as he climbed a poorly lit staircase. I could hear Chris's heavy breath rasping behind me.

Three men sat on mats around a low table in a dimly lit room. They looked haggard. Chris lay down on a mat in the corner. She was shivering. Reddish lamplight cast shadows on sandy walls. I shared another pipe with the men and stared at the ground between my feet. An industrious ant marched in a circle on the floor. I felt isolated. The ant went round and round in a pointless circle. No one said a word. The ant went round again, in ever decreasing circles. Chris looked like she was dead and I didn't fucking care. I was buzzing. The ant went round again and again and again.

That ant was my last memory. The last memory until a one-eyed man woke me. He pushed his foot against my head. Chris was moaning. A coal-dark man had a bunch of her hair in his hand. There was a knife against her throat.

I leapt up, but One-eye kicked me and I crashed onto the floor, smashing my jaw. Someone growled in Arabic. Coal-man pulled Chris's money belt from beneath her waistband and cut through it with his knife. There wasn't much in it. I had all the traveller's cheques. The man spat on the floor in disgust. I stared up at One-eye's empty socket.

"Open," he said, kicking at my money belt.

One-eye counted the cheques, held them up to the light.

"Go. Fetch Dirham," he said. "Ten thousand. Back before night. No Police." As the one-eyed guy spoke, Coal-man drew his blade, ever so slowly, across Chris's neck. A crimson bead trickled towards her T-shirt.

"Don't leave me, Manny!" she screamed.

I was cold and disorientated. My jaw ached. I followed my instincts and walked in a zigzag. I found the souk. From there, it was a short walk to the bank. I shuffled from one foot to the other, waiting for it to open. I cashed every single cheque. Then I rolled a joint and sucked hard on it, like I'd suffocate if I stopped.

I headed towards the narrow building, but when I reached the souk, I realised I had absolutely no idea where it was. The card. I needed the card. The 'Tiger Carpets' card had the address on it. I'd beat the shit out of that bastard Mustapha, if he didn't take me straight to his short-arsed friend. I opened the brown bag. The carpet twinkled like a soft jewel. Nothing. I spread the carpet out on the ground and tipped my bag out onto it. I checked my money belt, pockets, everything. No card. No address.

I rolled another joint. That's when I found the remains of the card in my hash tin. I'd used it for the roach. The address was gone.

And that's when the devil tapped me on the shoulder.

~

I came back home months later, hollow-eyed and underweight. I had the stupid carpet, but very little else. The story I told the police in Tangier was partly true. We *had* been held captive and robbed. But I never said how I left Chris to go find *the real Morocco* on my own.

A few months ago, Eleanor and I were in a thrifty store in Kingston, looking for clothes pegs or some shit.

"Look," she said. "Those carpets. They're the same as the tatty one we've got in the lounge."

My heart did a crazy dance.

It was the size of a bathmat, but beautiful. Like the pattern on a dragonfly's wing, laced with peacock iridescence. I ran my finger through its deep pile. Blues and golds. Turquoise and velvet.

I fingered the label, 'Made in Taiwan'.

I found the price tag. How much did it cost? How much was a life worth?

Five pounds. Just five sodding pounds, reduced from eight.

Words Around Two Mothers

I've known her for years. Her son was one of those skinny kids who shrank into himself. The boy was in the same class at school as my son. He didn't say much.

When they became friends and wanted sleepovers, the mother visited my husband and me. I liked that about her — the fact that she looked around our house like a detective, searching for clues, looking for anything that might harm her boy before leaving him with us.

I liked many things about her. That's why we became friends. Like me, she loved the theatre. We were both teachers. We liked classical music and hated gardening. She invited me to productions at The Adelphi and The Court. We'd have a wine afterwards.

After my husband left me, my friend helped pick through the carnage. She pieced the vestiges of what remained of me together again. She'd feed me wine to anaesthetise the pain. I'd fall asleep on her couch, waking the next morning covered by a blanket, my spiky heels and handbag stacked in the corner.

She'd lend me a pair of trainers and we'd walk the hills. The wind would blow my hangover away. We'd talk, her son trotting ahead of us, his daypack bobbing up and down on his shoulders. She'd coach me on singledom.

The boy's mother was an expert in the field. She knew what it was to have been abandoned.

I'd leave feeling lighter, but that levity would disappear whenever I arrived at my ex-husband's to collect my boy.

My ex's new partner was young. The worst thing about her was that she was *nice*. Her *niceness* grated more than her pert breasts. I couldn't help staring at them, imagining my ex's hands over her skin. I burned with jealousy. I wanted to hate her.

Things improved as my son grew older and more independent. I didn't see as much of them, though they lived close by. They'd chosen their house carefully so our son didn't have far to travel between his two homes and school. By fourteen, he was biking there and back on his own, only there wasn't much *back*.

He preferred staying with his father.

It maddened me, but I didn't want confrontation. I don't know why my son gravitated there. Perhaps it was a man thing, boys and their fathers. Maybe it was the wife's baking; French pastries and bosomy bread.

I was alone a lot. I'd call my friend. She'd listen.

I went on a handful of dates with people I met through *Friends of The Adelphi* and an on-line dating site. But things rarely progressed.

"I'd like to be friends," one said, with a subtext of *nothing more*.

"It's been lovely," another announced as we split the bill, his eyes telling me it hadn't been quite lovely enough.

Others were bolder. "I'm looking for something different."

I wasn't ready. They could smell the disappointment in me, the shame of being an abandoned wife.

So I spent more time with my friend. She became my main ally. Sure, I had other mates, but none of them understood me as she did. My friend anticipated what I would say before an idea left my lips.

I made her laugh.

When we played board games, we were competitive, but each gave the other chances, so there was never a clear winner; we were always so close.

We visited secondhand shops with the boys and came home with sacks of treasure: toys for the kids; chiffon scarves and grotesque hats for the two of us, all for less than twenty dollars.

If I was sad, she showed love by making little gifts – homemade shortbread in cellophane bags tied with curled ribbons, cards with silly cartoons to make me smile.

When she needed someone, I was there for her, whether it was to help replace a flat tyre or hold a ladder while she cleaned the gutters.

Then I killed our friendship.

~

If you ask me why I did it, I could make excuses.

I was lonely. I needed the attention. I had a moment of insanity.

My actions broke our bond.

Can people know things they haven't seen? Did she smell the guilt I radiated?

She can't have known, because she would have killed me if she'd found out. She would have torn the organs from my body. She can't have known, and yet something soured between us after I committed my crime.

I guess there are things you can see in a person, through their skin, through their lies. Through their shame. My shame.

She knew things would never be the same between us, though she had no idea what had unleashed the demon that killed our friendship.

I knew it was over too.

I knew it the morning after I'd seduced her fifteen-year-old son.

I miss her warmth, the two of us laughing, the way she would tell me everything would be all right. Lord knows, I need someone to show me how this thing with her son is going to end, to tell me it will all be fine. I can't talk to anybody about it. But I don't want to talk to just *anybody*.

I want to talk to my friend.

And I know I never can.

The Lemon Lover

I once loved a man who couldn't get hard unless he'd smothered his cock in lemon juice.

Before I met Max, I'd believed *lemon fetish* was an artisan cheese, feta-like and slightly crumbly. Otto discovered it in a deli when we were touring Canada. But then, it was so like Otto to fall in love with a mild-mild cheese. Me, I'm an *Epoisse de Bourgogne* man – a cheese so pungent it is banned on public transport in France.

Otto and I are like chalk and cheese. He's vanilla to my wasabi. And yes, that is a fair comparison. I first tasted a pale green wasabi-flavoured ice cream when Otto and I were in New York around 2002. (You can guess what flavour he chose.) I am tattooed with piercings. He is plain and unadorned. But I digress. Maybe it is the chalky-cheesiness of our relationship that has kept Otto and I together for almost thirty years. How long have we been together now? I'm losing count. But see, I've digressed again.

Back to Max.

Oof!

His habit added a certain zest to our fucking. Max was a Top. Exclusively. I'd go home after our trysts and snuggle up to Otto, yet complain of a headache if he misinterpreted my proximity for friskiness.

"I don't know what you're asking for, Zeb," he'd moan.

Headache – schmedache. The reality was the acid bite of Max's dick would leave me sore, but had me feeling scandalously horny; a cruel combination.

I found Max on *Splodge.org,* the same site where I'd found David. But you'll hear more about David later. Max and I met seven or eight times over the summer of 2018. One time, we added a half blind Chinese btm to the mix. The btm status helped with Max being exclusively Top. The guy was beautiful. I'd lusted after him ever since I'd seen his profile the previous November. That session ended in tears – literally – the btm got lemon in his good eye. It wasn't the best of my Max liaisons. Though threesomes (or more) are fun, and appeal to the list-ticker in me, I actually prefer to experience my men one at a time. I crave the intimacy.

Why? You're probably asking why, since I have a husband at home. But though Otto and I are intimate (not often, but we are), I need more than he can provide. I want variety, but I want to get close to each person. I want to hear their soft whispers. I want to know what makes them happy and what frightens them. I want to share my deepest fantasies with them, even though there's a chance I may never see them again, *especially* as there's a chance I may never see them again. To use a cliché, you could say I'm a serial monoandrist. I suppose I let myself fall a little in love with each man when I'm with him. Well, most of them, anyway.

Let me tell you about my final encounter with Max. It didn't end with a big bang, more a pathetic whimper.

Max was feeling fragile. A friend of his had had a near death experience that involved an unhappy combination of Viagra and poppers. Max wanted me to hold him. Nothing else. The lemons sat in his bag on the floor beside the bed, untouched, a small paring knife poking through the partly open zipper like an accusation.

I *wanted* to be there for Max, but fuck it, I was paying for the day use hotel room, and I wasn't going to waste my money. Plus I was wearing my new Cellblock 13 flasher body harness, and I felt a bit of a twat sweating in it under the covers. What a waste.

Although I didn't have a sore bot, I was grumpy as I walked home. I planned to hop into the shower so I could take care of myself, but Otto accosted me as soon as I walked through the door.

"Zeb! You're back. Where were you? Anyway, you're just in time." He untied his apron. "Anniversary dinner's about to go on the table. Do you want to go get washed?"

Washed? Did I stink? Could he smell rubber? The idea of having a *soothing* shower was less appealing than it had been five minutes earlier. Otto had remembered our anniversary and I'd forgotten. The combination of guilt and frustration made me doubly uncomfortable, and a knot of shame kept working its way up my throat.

~

Otto is a great cook. As I dried myself, stomach rumbling (I'd skipped lunch), I wondered what he'd prepared. But as my husband brought each course to the table, my paranoia lurched into overdrive. Surely he'd discovered what I'd been up to? He'd used lemon in everything. Lemon wedges pushed between scampi fritters. Moroccan chicken with preserved lemon slices scattered on our plates. Citrus tart decorated with crystallised lemon.

Did Otto have an idea what I'd been up to with Max? Was he about to challenge me?

I waited.

Nothing happened, apart from small talk about whether we should buy a food dehydrator. We finished our tart. I asked for seconds. Otto fetched me some from the kitchen. There was half a cucumber on the counter, and I'd almost expected him to bring it in and bash me over the head with it. But all Otto did was serve me a second slice of tart and have more himself.

The idea that he knew what I'd done, and was punishing me through a surfeit of pleasure was strangely intoxicating. Yet how could Otto have found out? I'd been so careful, planning false work shifts when I had my secret days off.

The food was delicious.

Shame I can't say the same about the sex that followed.

But you can't have everything.

Appetite

When Jennifer goes hunting, she wants flesh. Meat packed in jeans and leather, with a gasoline taint.

Jennifer's children stay with their grandmother, who plants anxious kisses on her daughter's cheek when she walks out of the door. Mother's eye tic and the bent line of her frown are measures of her silent disapproval. Jennifer is to collect the children on time, so her mother won't be late for Sunday matins.

Jennifer stakes out her territory in mini-skirted obscurity. The corrosive acidity of one-too-many-a-drink and the unwanted attention of a predator with the wrong sort of eyes do nothing to slow her.

The metallic drum of desire beats in her head, and Jennifer makes her choice.

She stumbles into steel-cold air. The mist of her breath mixes with a beer-cloud dancing on the stranger's lips.

He grapples with elastic as they fall into a taxi. They kiss in hungry gasps. The whale of desire threatens to swallow her whole. Cigarettes and forgotten vomit. Unwashed fever and the sausage tang of his breath. The driver clicks to Bollywood beats, unaffected by the gasps behind him.

At Jennifer's house, the sheets are cold, but everything else is burning.

They make it into the bed just in time.

When it is over, Jennifer leaves him comatose in the unkempt bed.

The linen is damp with sweat and disappointment.

She tiptoes over discarded clothes and toys to fix a drink, to fix her life. Her fingers are slick with the essence of another human being. Jennifer's lips tremble as she lights a cigarette. The buzz of her laptop stirs the air, as she taps the keys. She updates her profile, states what she wants in a lover.

She dreams of escape, and hopes.

When Words Alone
Are Not Enough

Looking back, you could say I fell in love for the first time at the age of twelve. You could also say what I felt toward my mother's friend Madeleine was anything *but* love.

~

I couldn't put a name to my emotions at that age. Neither did I have words to describe my reaction three years later, when I discovered Madeleine felt the same about me.

My first memory of her is when I was younger. Three of us running along Brighton beach: Madeleine, her son Kyle and me tugging at our kites. I guess I'd always had those soaring feelings around her. But aged nine, when Kyle was my best friend, I thought I was simply happy to be away from the constant bickering I faced at home.

Kyle and I had fun. We liked designing comics and laughing at each other's stupid jokes.

Our mothers were close too. They became inseparable when Kyle's father left Madeleine and took up with a young French woman who had tits like Hershey's Kisses. Kyle had just turned twelve. Guess Madeleine identified with Mum: another woman left to catch the baby while the daddy played away, only *my* father had disappeared before I was born.

Mum would soothe Madeleine with a shared bottle of fizz. That was when I noticed the bow of her lips, and how she looked prettier, not hideous as most women do, when she cried.

I couldn't describe my emotions back then. They'd become unstoppable though formless. They only took shape under my sheets, where they had to be wiped away afterwards.

I saw less of Kyle as we reached puberty. Though he was a month older, I was way ahead of him. Our mothers carried on meeting without us.

Sometimes Madeleine stayed over after too many wines. I'd creep out and look at her in the grey dawn light, watch the rise and fall of her chest in time with her almost silent breathing. I'd take in her scent, the semi-visible glow of her hair, and hope she'd never go away.

But I always knew she'd have to leave in the morning.

Maybe it was love. Something raw and primeval. Maybe it was something else. I wanted to be with her. But I also wanted to hurt Madeleine, because she stopped me from being whole. Bits of me followed her when she left. I wouldn't find them until I was near her again.

Was it normal to hate the person you love?

Madeleine came away with Mum and me the summer before my sixteenth birthday. Kyle was in France with his father. He was spending more time with Abe than with his mother. She was lonely. We stayed at a beach hut in Taylor's. The ocean thrashed and roared and kept you awake at night, but I didn't mind. I loved that place. I loved it even more after what happened that holiday. The touch of Madeleine on my skin, the softness of her lips, the fearful excitement of keeping our love hidden, because though we never spoke the word, that's what I believed it was. Love.

And then what?

I'd wanted her for so long, I wasn't sure what to do when Madeleine became my lover. Sometimes she was tender. Other times she'd push me away, tell me what we were doing was wrong. Then she'd become needy and desperate.

I was confused.

Her neighbour saw me leaving late one night. Questions were asked.

"This has to stop, Ronan." The creases on Madeleine's forehead told me she meant it. "You should start seeing girls your own age."

I followed her advice.

Our separation lasted two months. I went back with stories about my teenage fumbling. She burned furious, unable to take back what she'd unleashed. I thrived on her jealousy. It must have meant she needed me.

~

Looking back, there was a particular moment when I could have ended it. That moment happened when I was on the cusp of adulthood.

~

We'd been drinking. The rain thrummed hard against the black window. I was supposed to be staying at a friend's house overnight. Not at Kyle's of course. I couldn't risk that. Besides, Kyle and I didn't mix in the same circles anymore. Madeleine and I had a full night together. She'd booked us into a hotel.

Stroking the down of my chest, she ventured into unknown territory: our future.

"Maybe we could start again in a different town," she said, "or another country."

And then what?

"Our ages are only numbers," she said. "Ours is the truest form of love." She cradled me, nuzzled me to her breast. I felt sick and rushed to the bathroom.

Sitting on the toilet lid, I studied the tiles under my feet.

She wouldn't know if I slipped away. I could grab my things and say I was going out for burgers. It had to be food, because I was too damn young to buy booze.

I could get away. The buses were still running. It would have to be a bus. I was too damn young to drive her car.

I was too damn young for all of it.

She'd be over fifty before I reached thirty.

I looked back once as I stepped into the rain, told myself I'd never go back. I was free. I just had to say the words.

Too fucking young.

But I was already thinking about parts of myself I'd left behind in that hotel.

I knew she'd be waiting for me.

~

Looking back, there was one moment I could have ended things with Madeleine. But I wasn't strong enough.

After so many years, we've lost so much. She has become an unbreakable habit.

I should have left her then. Because now, even though I'm old enough to know better, older, yet no wiser, I know I'll never be able to let her go.

The Night My Sister Leaves

The night my sister leaves, electrons are brushed from their moorings and the air fizzes with anticipation.

I know what's going to happen. I know about the leather case in the gap between the brick wall and lavender hedging. Yet it is me whom others see as dishonest.

I lie about the size of things, and am regarded as untrustworthy.

My sister is allergic to nut-butters. She avoids touching knives. At night she sucks the space around us, our beds adjacent like parallel coffins. The room is dark, wet with our dreams, our fears slick as oil. She is growing into a woman, while I am encased in a child's skin.

I am frightened of the gaps between darkness. She is scared of not being loved.

My sister has asked to borrow our mother's coat. She says she's going to a friend's party.

I'll be back by eleven, don't wait up.

I know she's not going to the party, but somewhere with harlequin lights and shady deals.

I am bound by secrecy. She will cut the tongue out of my body if I tell.

But I had to be told, because we share a room, and I see more than I ought.

The night my sister leaves, I am painting my aunt's figure in watercolours. My hair is a mess, my homework unfinished.

My sister walks out of the door, and I'm uncertain whether I imagine a silky tail swishing from thigh to thigh beneath the hem of my mother's coat. It might be the slinkiness of her dress.

I lick the tip of my brush. My uncle smiles at the prominence of his wife's lips, her cracks shrunk to fault-lines beneath the skin.

It's been six months since my aunt left. She took the baby with her.

He recognises her.

Everyone else sees only patterns.

My brother wraps a chocolate piece between slices of cold potato. There's a blood-blister on the tip of his finger that I want to lick, but stare at him instead. He chews like a machine, tells me my painting disobeys the laws of physics.

"But it's more fun than science," I say, and my father asks if I have done my homework.

"No."

He grunts without opening his mouth, lips like twin caterpillars beneath his moustache. So I tip the paint-water into the kitchen sink and sit in the dormant shadow of my mother as she cooks. Reciting equations under my breath,

I shout at the absurdity of sub-atomic particles.

"What are cations?" my mother asks.

"They're like lions, but with less fur," I tell her. My lie is absorbed into the atmosphere of dishonesty and malaise.

When I'm done, my mother pulls my abundant hair into a ponytail and shows me the alchemy of baking. We make buns for my grandmother. It's her birthday, and she won't eat anything with egg in it.

Later we talk about viruses and hobgoblins. I tell my grandmother they are roughly the same size. I like to fill her head full of lies. Head lies.

The cat, as fat as a macaroon, licks imaginary cream off itself, while my father complains about the importance of a good education and shakes his fist at the television, unaware that his eldest daughter will be knocking back vodka in the arms of a passing sailor. My mother's coat will be ruined.

I lie about the size of things, and am regarded as untrustworthy. So when I find my sister is missing from her bed that night, I shrink her absence into something that cannot be measured.

I close my eyes until morning.

Morning.

Birds explode in the sky like myths.

My sister has not come back. The case has gone. This is the first day of the rest of our incomplete lives.

For now, the house has a full set of chromosomes in every brick.

D/F

David Qureshi had an alter ego.

I found David *and* Fatima on *Splodge.org.*

I hadn't specifically been looking for someone composed of two parts, but that's how Qureshi came (so to speak).

D/F made it to my 'shortlist'. He was one of the men I went back to, someone I could temporarily fall in love with and then let go when I wanted to slip back to easy domesticity with my husband Otto.

Otto was married to a woman before he was with me. He had three children with his ex-wife. He stayed with Hazel while the children were young, sustaining his other inclinations by means of trips to the sauna. That's where I met him. It's where I found most of the men I fucked in those days, before sites such as *Splodge.org* were invented.

I once asked Otto to describe the heterosexual sex act to me. I was curious. Sure, I'd had a few fumbling kisses and gropes with girls at school, but it had always felt wrong, something akin to incest. Otto had loved his wife, though I don't think he's truly bisexual. What he described with Hazel neither turned my stomach, nor did it turn me on. It just satisfied my curiosity. He described it as poached eggs against hard-boiled (with the shell on). I'd never wanted to try poached. Until I met D/F.

When D/F was in Fatima mode, she was 99.9% woman. Her mannerisms were feminine, as was the way she spoke, and even how she smelled. There were anatomical 'inaccuracies' of course, but I wouldn't have wanted it any other way. We usually met in a day use hotel room. But when the hotels were closed, D/F invited me to his/her apartment. Those liaisons were the best, because that's where Zorah made an appearance.

I'd turn up in leather trousers and biker jacket, though the nearest I'd been to riding a motorbike was with Ham on the motorway. He'd scared the crap out of me. I'd clutched his waist and thought I was going to die. But you'll hear more about Ham later.

I'd walk through D/F's door as Zeb, and (s)he would transform me into Zorah.

We were lucky in that D/F and I shared the same shoe size. It meant I had the choice of heels, flats, strappy sandals and boots. The boots were the best.

I've never considered myself a cross-dresser. I'm confident about who I am. I know my gender identity and sexuality. But even a straight-laced gay guy has his quirks. David/Fatima was an outlet for my quirkiness.

I was slightly broader in the shoulder than D/F, so some of the zippered tight-fitting gowns were impossible. But there was a stretchy sequinned number that worked. It showed my arse off nicely.

Fatima would share her make-up, blackening my eyes with liner, and softening the contours of my face with concealer and magic. She was a true artist, though I had to be doubly careful to scrub my skin before I left the place. Some things are harder to lie my way out of with Otto than others.

Take prophylaxis for example.

I'd started PrEP by the time I met D/F. We enjoyed bareback. The meds were necessary for my rediscovered 'hobby'. Oh, I haven't always been as slutty as I am now. Otto and I have had periods of exclusivity. It's just that they haven't lasted very long. But taking the tablets has proven problematic at times. Waiting for a discreet opportunity, sometimes I'd forget a dose altogether. I'd end up frotting and playing safe in other ways until I knew I was protected again.

But I digress.

Fatima and Zorah went out clubbing. We only did it once. I felt too vulnerable to make a habit of it. Not that anyone would have recognised me under the auburn wig. I also wore sunglasses and a mask in the taxis on the way there and back to the apartment. It doesn't hurt to be careful. Someone Otto knows goes to places like that. I wouldn't trust them not to say anything. I kept looking over my shoulder all evening. Fatima and I drank cocktails. We danced around our handbags – I'd borrowed a beaded purse that went well with the sequinned dress. We had a good time, though my feet were sore afterwards.

~

I must have seen David/Fatima over a period of about six months. It was almost a relationship, though he did have an actual long-term partner for the duration. And I had Otto.

Then D/F stopped responding to my 'come-fuck-me' messages. I knew where he lived, of course, but I never went there. It wouldn't have been right.

Afterwards, I had an on and off thing with an undertaker in his forties. He was married to a woman and had two young children.

Then I slipped back into 'mix'n'match'.

Sometimes Otto asks whether I'm happy with our relationship. It's not that he's questioning it. He's just that sort of person. He likes to check.

"Yes, of course," I tell him. Otto is good to me. But he's boring as fuck at times. There are things I still haven't tried during my time on the planet. Otto would never do them. I've asked. He's even squeamish about my tongue piercing.

But I want to try them. I need an outlet for other aspects of my quirky side.

"Yes," I tell him. "I wouldn't want things any other way."

And it's true. It's easy with Otto.

If I had a possessive clingy husband, how would I ever do everything I needed?

Otto does his thing: tending to the garden, bottling fruit, designing jackets.

And I do mine.

It's just that he tells me more about his activities than I ever tell him about mine.

Getting the Story Right

Burt Hartley saw a boy in school uniform creep out of my house at dawn's first light. It was the second week of December. My neighbour put two and two together, concluded a schoolboy leaving the house at five a.m. didn't add up; especially as the boy wasn't my son.

He took things further and changed my life forever.

Burt should have been asleep at that hour, but he was a nosey bastard, all twitching curtains and eyes wide as grapes peering over the fence. Though it was none of his business, he wanted to know why a boy was pushing his bicycle through my front gate that summer morning. I tried to get the story right, but Burt's suspicions eventually led to the culmination of my twenty-year-long teaching career.

Those twenty years haven't been easy.

Living in an earthquake-affected city was hard. The demolitions, dust and rebuilds affected the kids I taught, and so they affected me. Then there was my divorce: the distance it created from my son. Kyle was always closer to his father, but I didn't expect him to choose Abe over me once he was old enough to take himself where he wanted to be.

My work became a source of stability and solace.

Teaching at Parkways wasn't easy. The high school doesn't serve the most affluent area. I loved the kids, even when they came with problems my son would never have faced. I liked the work despite its challenges. What I did made a difference.

Now I've lost everything, because of Burt fucking Hartley.

Ronan was supposed to leave while it was dark, not so easy as the shortest night of the year loomed. When my alarm woke us we'd had sex again and fallen into a deep sleep.

Murky light penetrated the curtains.

"Shit!" I shoved him. "You've got to go."

"What? What time is it?"

"Almost daylight." I pushed him out of bed. "Go. Now!"

We lived on the boundary between different zones. Most kids on our street sported the maroon-trimmed uniform Ronan and Kyle wore. Some dressed in motley Parkways colours. One wore the striped blazer of a fee-paying school.

Ronan pulled his uniform on.

"Sorry," I whispered. "Love you."

He grunted a reply. He might have said he loved me. He could just as easily have been swearing. Tripping over his own feet, he knocked a chair against the wall.

"Quiet!" I whispered, but he was sex-drunk and clumsy as he left my bedroom.

I watched him through the window. The sky was growing paler. He dropped his bike lock with a clatter. Burt's curtain moved, sending shafts of blue-white light across his lawn. I mouthed an insult my neighbour would never hear.

After he left, I ached for Ronan. It had never been like that with Abe or any of the louche men I'd dated after my husband left me. Ronan occupied my thoughts. Fully.

Picking up a pile of crumpled papers, I started marking assignments that were due in a few days.

Burt questioned me when I was leaving for work.

"Who was coming out of your house this morning?"

I dug into my handbag for car keys.

"No one," I said. "Why do you ask?"

"I saw him," Burt continued. "A child."

The bag slipped from my shoulder. "Who?" Essays slipped onto the path.

"A boy."

"If you think there was an intruder, call the police. Give a description."

I'd used similar tactics with my pupils when they crossed me. Suggesting something ludicrous sometimes made them back off.

Tell the whole class, you two. Louder, so we can all hear.

Write a formal complaint to the head teacher, and tell him his rule is out-dated.

Wear your skirt even shorter, so we can see everything when you bend over.

"I *will* be reporting this to the police, Madeleine," Burt said, "only you didn't have no intruder last night."

Gathering the papers, I considered correcting Burt's use of the double negative, but decided not to.

Things escalated fast. The accusation?

Abusing a position of authority and trust.

The head hauled me into his office the following day.

"Where's the proof?" I demanded.

"The photograph shows a boy in school uniform."

"Photo?" Burt had taken pictures. Bastard. A fucking scheming one at that.

"With a maroon trim," my boss continued.

I wanted to say it was none of his business. *Different school. No position of authority.* But instead, I denied it.

There was more. We'd been seen. Some of the accusations had substance. Others were just rumour.

It took the best part of a year before I was forced to resign.

For what? I hadn't hurt anyone.

You see cases in the media: a balding maths teacher, a desperate girl. She has no friends, no self-esteem. He grooms her. He breaks the trust between the girl and her parents. He becomes her sole focus.

I didn't do that with Ronan.

I simply fell in love.

Friends shunned me. Ronan's mother Jacqui was the first to drop me. Perhaps as a teacher herself, she found it hard to accept someone in the profession might do such a thing. And yet – if she'd known …

Burt's blurry picture had revealed an unidentifiable schoolboy. If Jacqui had guessed it was Ronan, she would have skinned me and incinerated the stripped flesh.

We'd been so careful, but not careful enough.

We're far more cautious now.

I have time, plenty of it. Still looking for work, I don't have money to spare, but I find ways to meet Ronan. There are abandoned properties around, even ten years after the earthquake. Dampness seeps into my back when we fuck, and I worry the rotten floor might collapse under us with the force of it.

Ronan will be a man soon.

He's going to take me away.

Those cases in the media: the balding teacher and the desperate girl.

We're nothing like that.

Ronan and I are in love.

The Sins of the Father

Anton called, and an image of baby booties sprang to mind. I broke into a grin.

"London? Yeah. I'll do it," I told the boss, trying to focus on what he was saying, though it was difficult with what was going through my head. The image of baby booties. Again.

The booties were the size of lamb's kidneys, made from flamingo-pink leather.

"Awesome," Anton replied. His Aussie drawl sounded strangely foreign, even though I'd only been away from work for a week.

"Yeah. No problem." I scratched my balls through the hotel dressing gown. "Can change my flights. Not an issue." I was standing at the window, phone cupped against my ear. The quayside lights reflected on the black of the river, sending blue and amber beams onto the darkened walls of the room. The banks of the Liffey always burst into life at night.

Anton outlined targets and goals. It was hard to imagine his stubbly chin and owl-glasses on the opposite side of the planet. It was difficult to home in on what he was saying. I had other things on my mind. I tried to picture how his day would have progressed so far. Anton would have cycled beside the lake in fluoro Lycra and changed into his shell-grey suit at work. I tried to concentrate as he outlined the extra assignment. I'd have nearly a week between both events. I noted the manufacturers I had to liaise with, tried to think whether there was anything else I needed from Anton, but the sodding image of baby booties wouldn't shift from my mind.

My boss must have realised I was distracted. He said he could offer the gig to Meryl, but the pink baby booties were fixed in my mind. I was staying put. I wanted that assignment.

"No. It's fine," I said. "Don't need to fly Meryl out here. I'll do it."

Anton outlined which products I needed to push to whatever clients. I caught a flash of red moving in the periphery of my vision and turned away from it. There was a faint roar, as if an asthmatic tiger had walked into the room. I ignored it.

I twisted to face the river again. Anton spoke of incentives and corporate gifts. I visualised my boss hanging his cycling shorts inside out on a peg next to his locker that morning, shorts complete with brown skid mark. His voice had a morning croak that told me he hadn't been up long. It was nine in the morning in Canberra. I imagined him sipping an espresso, rubbing his eyes with the back of his wrist the way he did.

"All right" I said. "I've got that." I blinked away the pinkness of the booties.

"That's great, Conor."

Those booties had been meant for me.

"No worries, mate," I said.

They were plastic-pink, reminiscent of Barbie kitchens and pony merchandise. The stuff little girls are made to believe they want.

"Meryl can fill you in," Anton continued. The asthmatic tiger growled again, finishing with a petulant hiss. "You'll stay in Dublin until next week, do you think? Or have a look around before you head to London?"

"I might — I might travel a bit. Around Ireland," I said.

Aunt Noreen had sent the booties to my parents when I was born.

"Sure. You've family in Ireland, right?"

"My Aunt Noreen. Haven't seen her for years. Some cousins." My bed looked warm and inviting. The growling had stopped, replaced by a wet slapping sound.

"So you'll visit them?"

My mother never once put those booties on me. But she kept them. Like she kept everything. My first trainers, my tricycle, my daycare centre sunhat. She kept my school workbooks, a lock of hair from my first haircut, and my second, and the third. The booties were still in their clear plastic box. As a kid, I'd asked why the booties were unworn. It was always the same answer.

"They were from your Aunt Noreen, but your father didn't want people thinking you were a girl," Mum had explained. Only when I was much older had I wondered why she hadn't thrown them out.

Daddy's little man.

Hundred percent manly man, like my father, that's what I was. There's a certain irony in that, knowing what I have become, even more so knowing what happened to him. Though at least I don't have any doubts about my masculinity. Zero.

The tiger called again. *I'm waiting, big boy. Rrrrrrr.*

"Yeah. I'll go see them," I told Anton and drew the blinds against the river, against the murmur from the street.

"You can put the travel down on your expenses," he said. "Since we're inconveniencing you."

"Cool." I stifled a giggle. It was difficult to concentrate with what was happening two paces away on my hotel bed.

Anton must have sensed I wasn't all there. He ended the call.

A volatile giggle bubbled in my throat.

An hour earlier, I'd swallowed a blue pill the boy with strawberry-red hair had given me. I'd met him in The George. He'd necked one himself and was now lying on my hotel bed, toying with his cock.

I forgot about Anton, and forgot about the baby booties. Gripping his bright red hair, I sank into the boy.

He roared in my ear.

Like a tiger.

Afterwards we went to Temple Bar – buskers, on every corner – people hustling for this and that. We lost ourselves in the wail of Uilleann pipes and chimes of a Chapman stick.

I bought the boy dinner. He chose a chicken breast wrapped in prosciutto with a green salad. I twirled tagliatelle with the fork in my right hand and stroked the redhead's inner thigh under the table with my left. Outside, we brushed away people touting for business. I watched the boy's breath take shape in the frigid air. Christmas lights flashed and music clashed. We had a drink at the PantiBar, danced for half the night at a party in Monto, and then I lost him, despite the traffic-light-red mane.

When I woke up, the sun was streaming through a gap in the blinds. I peered at my watch. Ten to two in the afternoon. I fell out of bed, and stumbled to the minibar. Twisting the cap off a water bottle, I drained the whole thing.

So. I had the best part of a week to do what the fuck I wanted. I didn't need to head to London until the following Sunday. Before then, I just had to make some calls, organise display stands, book caterers, and then the rest of the time was mine. All mine.

I wanted to see my family.

I guess that's what the baby booties had been about. I wanted to visit Aunt Noreen. I hadn't seen her since I was five. Most of my impressions of my aunt were drawn from photographs and stilted long-distance phone calls as a child. I couldn't remember when I'd last spoken to her or Uncle Pat. I didn't know what they were doing, or even where they lived. I needed to see them, to know all my relatives weren't as screwed up as my immediate family.

When I lived with Ma, I'd absorb family news from her. People sent Christmas cards back then. Mum would file Noreen's festive message in a cupboard with tattered old teddy bears, Christening robes, collections of milk teeth, and a pair of flamingo-pink baby shoes.

The snaps Noreen sent showed cousins Diarmuid and Sinead staring out from the white-bordered prints, the Irish light different from the brutal Canberra sun that burns welts into your skin. Noreen's letters told Mum who'd died, who'd separated, who'd married, and who'd done the unthinkable.

When he lived with us, my father would shout at Mum, tell her to *throw all that garbage out.* Her boxes spilled onto floors, into corridors, filled the garage, made every room into an obstacle course. She shuffled things about, to create the illusion she was doing something with all that crap, in order to placate my father.

When Noreen sent the baby shoes, I don't know if she hadn't registered I was a boy, or didn't give a shit about colour coding. But in their box they remained. Untouched. Ma had asked if I wanted to take them when I last saw her. She'd said she was having a clear out. I'd been hopeful. Someone, probably me, would have to chuck everything out when she carked. But it hadn't been the first time she'd had good intentions, only to replace all the crap with other *potentially useful* things, as soon as a space was cleared.

"God knows, Conor," she'd said, while flicking

through my school reports and packing my father's old eyeglasses into a zip lock bag for charity, "you won't have kids of your own, but you should keep these." The accusation hung in the air like cordite. I was the only child, a child destined not to procreate through choice.

I'd taken the booties. They were a link to the Kavanagh part of me I might otherwise have lost.

I opened the minibar again. Miniature whiskeys and cans of beer rattled for my attention. I ignored them and tore open a pack of peanuts.

If I wanted to see Aunt Noreen, I had to find her first. My scant memories of my aunt were of a tall woman with the same broad forehead as I had, but with more hair. She shared the Kavanagh skull most of us had.

I had some of my cousins as social media contacts. I didn't know whether they lived in Ireland anymore. However, half an hour after I messaged him, my cousin Diarmuid sent me his parents' contact details, filled me in on who'd given birth, divorced, died or gone to prison. It was the first time I'd contacted him in years. He bombarded me with news and questions. Diarmuid tagged pictures of his wife and children, and asked if I had married, now that I could.

Now that I could? Seems my cousin kept abreast of news from *our* family. He knew my preferences and the political persuasions of our country when it came to same sex unions, late though it was in coming. But he didn't know the abhorrence I felt at the thought of settling down with just one person.

Thanking him for the updates, I didn't answer any of his questions. His parents still lived in the west. I could be there in less than three hours by train.

Unsurprisingly, my aunt didn't recognise me when I called.

"It's me. Conor."

She'd likely not heard my voice since it had broken.

"Ay? Conor from Murphy's?"

"No." I said. "Conor Kavanagh. Your nephew."

"Frankie's boy? Is that you?"

I bristled at the mention of his name.

"Yeah. I'm over from Australia." I threw my clothes into the hard-shelled case as we spoke. Considered wearing the Armani, so it wouldn't crease in a suit bag.

"Oh. *Conor,*" she spoke my name as if I had a disease.

"I'd like to come and see yous."

"See us?"

It wasn't the welcome I'd hoped for.

"I'm in Ireland for work. Got some spare time." An image of Anton's owl-eye spectacles and soiled cycling shorts flashed through my mind. I pushed the image away.

"Work. Is that so?"

"Look if you're busy − or if it's inconvenient, I'll leave it."

"I didn't say that." The ice in her words melted a little, but not much. I wondered why she'd sent the baby booties when I'd been born. It didn't seem in keeping with her current disinterest. But then all babes are innocent. I thought about calling the whole thing off and heading to The George again. Perhaps my redheaded tiger would be there. My groin pulsed like a fresh bruise at the thought. Even if he weren't, there would be plenty more candy to chose from.

"I just thought – " I didn't push it. Maybe I'd made a mistake. Perhaps my aunt wasn't as liberal as my cousin. Homophobia and binary thinking rear their ugly heads in many ways. Pink leather booties? Maybe she *had* thought I was a girl when I was born, though there sure as hell aren't many girl's names that sound like Conor.

Honor?

Caragh?

Cleona?

Nah.

"No, Conor. It'd be a pleasure to have you," her tone had changed. "When are you thinking of coming?"

I vacillated. Had I imagined her earlier reserve?

"I'm in Dublin. I was thinking of getting the train," I hesitated. I had thought of going later that afternoon, but something made me change my mind. I'd stay in the city another night. I chucked the Armani back on a hanger and pulled my leather trousers from the case. "I could come tomorrow on the four o'clock. It gets in at six fifteen."

"That'll be grand. You know where we are now? Pat and I can come fetch you."

"I'll make my own way. Look forward to seeing you, Aunt Noreen."

"You too, Conor. See you tomorrow."

It was getting dark. There were two tiny bottles of whiskey in the minibar. Anton was pretty good about covering expenses. I twisted both caps off, tipped the contents into a tumbler, added water and drained it, then got ready. The bald guy staring from the mirror looked older than me, reminded me of my father. Crap. Wisps of regrowth had appeared above the ears. I shaved my head so it shone like a wet stone. Though baldness was supposedly a sign of virility, with my prominent forehead, I looked like Montgomery Burns from the Simpsons if I wasn't clean-shaven. I took a beer from the fridge.

The bars would start filling soon. I stepped into the crisp cold air, and set out for The George. A pair of drag queens walked out as I approached, all pneumatic bosoms and synthetic wigs. I spat on the ground, waited until they'd gone before entering.

A guy with tight curls and obsidian skin approached me. I liked the way he moved.

"What are you drinking?" he asked. His eyes held a warmth I found appealing. The night was showing promise. I could smell excitement in the air.

I reached the station on Monday afternoon as indigo streaks etched the sky. I'd have expected the train to be fuller so close to Christmas. But as I heaved my case into the luggage rack, I found plenty of empty seats. I'd opted for a late check out from the hotel that morning, and kicked the guy with blue-black skin out half-an-hour ahead of me, then showered and slipped into my suit. I hadn't wanted anyone to see us leave together.

My eyes danced across the pages of my book, some story about a bisexual guy in love with a straight man. I couldn't concentrate. So I closed the book and allowed myself to drift into the memory of charcoal black fingers slipping against mine. When I'd held the man in my arms, I'd wondered if it was possible to love someone. To *really* love someone, so you'd never let them slip away.

It was raining and the leaden sky was turning black when I lugged my case onto the platform. Someone immediately slipped their fingers onto the handle. A separate pair of arms folded around me from behind.

"Conor!"

Relief followed a microsecond of panic as my cousin's wife kissed my cheek. Her scent reminded me of peaches.

"This is Annie. We're parked not far from here." Diarmuid hugged me again, a bold, strong hold. "Haven't seen you since you were, oh I don't know, that high?" He flattened his palm against his boy's chin. "This is Eamonn. And here's Niamh." The small girl from Diarmuid's Facebook pictures slipped her hand into mine.

"Can you play *Bug Trails* with us, Uncle Conor?"

"Let's get out of this weather first." Her father nudged the child forward. The rain pounded harder as Annie drove us away from the station.

"Do you like Pokémon?" the girl asked, reaching across from her car seat and pulling the sleeve of my Armani. I hoped her fingers were clean. Diarmuid leaned back from the front passenger's seat and ruffled the girl's hair. "Thought we'd head to Ma and Da's, have a bite to eat. When Sinead arrives, we'll head to Jerry Flannery's for a drink, if you like. They have a live band on." He smiled, and my cousin's Kavanagh forehead reminded me of Dad. I had to look away.

"Is it morning in Australia?" the boy asked. I looked at my watch, thought about Anton pushing his bike out of the dark garage where his wife kept her car.

"Yeah. People are heading for work."

"Really?"

"And it's hot. *So* hot."

"Summer?"

"Yeah." I settled back into the seat, stretched my arms behind me head. Family. Wasn't this what I'd wanted? Wasn't this what I'd missed for years?

Annie pulled into a driveway. Fairy lights twinkled from a front window. Uncle Pat approached and opened the car door. He looked much older than I remembered, and not as tall. He shook my hand and then slapped my back as I left the car. The children scattered like skittles into the house. I followed. A meaty aroma blew out from the door, and I remembered I hadn't eaten anything since I'd licked whipped cream from a spray can off the blue-black man's skin. How many hour's ago was that?

"Is she here yet? Is she here?" Niamh shouted and ran through to her grandmother. I stepped in from the rain and looked into Aunt Noreen's eyes. They were filled with tears. The image of the pink booties came into my head, and a surge of emotion almost knocked me over.

"Oh, would you look at you? You're the absolute image of − " but my aunt didn't finish her sentence. She just held me. Niamh tugged at her cardigan.

"Is she *here*?" the girl cried, barely able to contain herself.

"Run along upstairs and have a look," my aunt said, and the child thundered up the carpeted steps shouting *Auntie Sinead, Auntie Sinead*. I breathed a sigh of relief as my aunt released me. Perhaps I'd been saved from *Bug Trails*, whatever that was.

"You're in here, mate," Diarmuid said, wheeling my case into a room to the left of the staircase. "Ma left you towels. Shower's at the end of the corridor if you want to freshen up before we eat."

Did I smell? I'd showered after kicking the guy out of the hotel that morning, but I imagined the acrid smell of numerous condoms had worked its way into my skin and was oozing from my pores. Perhaps my cousin could smell the essence of man on me. The thought unnerved me. Before I could say anything further, my uncle led me into the lounge. I shoved the enormous box of Butler's chocolates I'd brought under the tree.

"Will you have a Jameson's, Conor?" My uncle placed the glass in my hand, as if he was instructing, not offering.

"Don't mind if I do," I said, rolling the first sip over my parched tongue.

Sinead walked in. She was prettier than I remembered. I could have gone for her if I'd liked that sort of thing, but it had been ten years since I'd last been with a woman. She took my hand.

"Hello, Conor," she said. Her voice was soft, and her palms cool.

"Time for tea," Aunt Noreen called from the hallway.

The days passed in a haze of trips to the castle, the cinema, pubs, restaurants and museums with Niamh and Eamonn. I didn't think about work. I didn't think about my mother. I laughed a lot. I didn't think about my father. From time to time, I thought about the man with blue-black skin, and was filled with a sense of regret. I didn't think about him enough though to wish I'd taken his number or e-mail.

I met other relatives I didn't know I had. They took me into their worlds as if I'd always belonged there.

I didn't want to leave.

It happened early on the Saturday morning. Aunt Noreen came into my room with a pile of laundry, neatly folded. My suit was suspended on a hanger from a peg on the back of the door.

The house was quiet. Diarmuid and Annie hadn't yet arrived. They didn't live far away. Sinead had gone for a run in O'Brien's Park. I guess I'd been waiting for it to happen all week, for the comfortable bubble of intimacy to burst and for them to expel me from their lives, like I was something from the trashcan.

Noreen sat on the bed, and patted the space next to her. Her face was drawn and the pouches under her eyes seemed darker than before. A flurry of wrinkles lined that great Kavanagh forehead. "We need to talk, Conor."

"About him?" The words slipped out of my mouth before I could stop them. "I'm not sure I want to." Maybe she'd not wanted to talk about *that*. Maybe she was worried about Pat's heart. Maybe she was fretting about the early arthritis restricting how much needlework she could do. Maybe it was the kids' eating habits, or it could have been about the price of vegetables. Maybe it was all of those things. But I knew it was none of them. And even though Aunt Noreen took her hand in mine, I felt her slip away from me. A pair of bright pink booties dissolved into nothing.

"About Frankie."

"I told you, I don't want to talk about him."

"No. Actually it's about *her*."

"That person is not part of my life anymore."

"Frankie loves you."

"He doesn't." My voice was like a child's. A hurt and abandoned child. A child who loved his father more than anybody in the world. A child destined to grow into an adult without the love of that father.

"You never gave her a chance."

"*He* never gave us a chance. Our family. You need to see – "

"No. You need to see, Conor. You need to open your eyes and see."

"You have no idea what it was like seeing Dad pretend to be a woman." I was shouting. I hadn't meant to.

"I can never know the pain you've been through, but

we have to move forward as a family." Noreen's tears ran down her cheeks and fell in wet patches on her cardigan.

"*Family!*" I let go of her hand and laughed in her face. "*Family?* Do you think he gave a shit about *family*, when he went ahead and did what he did?"

"I know it was hard for you."

"*Hard for me?* Can you even hear yourself, Noreen?"

"I'm trying to understand."

"No one can understand. No one else has been through what I've experienced."

"Talk to me about it, Conor."

"I can't. I can't talk to anyone about it. There was a time I could have, I would have. But I didn't have anyone to talk to then. Don't you get it? That young boy is dead." My voice was almost gone.

"Oh, Conor."

"My mother wouldn't listen. Lost in her little world. Collecting shit in boxes, cataloguing, hoarding. She's got a fucking disease, and no one sees it." I wiped a line of snot on my shirtsleeve. At least I didn't have my suit on.

"Oh, Conor."

"Stop." I raised my palm to her. "Stop saying *Oh Conor*, as if anything you say makes a difference."

"I don't know what to say. I know you're hurting. You're hurting *so* much."

"*Hurting?* You don't know the half of it. Do you know what it was like? Do you know how your brother destroyed our family? Do you think my mother was crazy like that before?"

"No, but — "

And even though it felt like I'd swallowed razor blades, I talked. I told my aunt about the daily beatings I took at school, when they found out about my dad.

At my school, you had to play rugby like a Wallaby, had to be funny or clever or all three. I was none of those things. I told Noreen how I'd grit my teeth and swear when they teased me about Dad.

I told my aunt how I'd lied about him, how I denied his existence. I would deny what he'd done until the kids beat the truth out of me, and made me say it, so there was no going back to a world where my father hadn't transitioned into a woman.

I told my aunt how they said I was like him, a pansy, a queer, a *shemale*. I told her how through it all, the only thing I was sure of was the fact that I was man, all man, but that I was a man who liked other men.

I told her how dirty that made me feel.

And then I cried in the arms of a woman I barely knew.

"I'm sorry you had to face what you did."

"It's not for you to be sorry, Aunt Noreen. It's for *him*. He's the only one who could have made it right. But he didn't."

"She loves you."

"He — he doesn't even look like one of us anymore. He's not even a Kavanagh anymore. That forehead vandalised by surgery. That awful wig. The way he flounces around in chiffons and silks."

"Frankie suffered too."

A car pulled into the driveway. A door slammed, followed by Niamh's happy screams.

"Uncle Conor!" She pounded the front door.

"Do you feel better for talking?" Noreen asked.

"No. No, I don't." It was cruel, like twisting a knife in my aunt's belly, but I wasn't sure anything could make me feel better. I looked into her wet eyes. "Tell me one thing."

"Yes?"

"Why did you send a pair of pink booties to Australia when I was born? Was it your idea of a joke? Did you know about Frank back then?"

"Nothing like that."

"What then?"

"I wanted my − my *brother* as he was then to know it was all right."

"*What* was all right?"

"For boys to have things that girls usually had. I did it for him."

"So you knew about him back then?"

"We all knew."

Aunt Noreen looked towards the door. The handle twisted. Eamonn and Niamh were arguing with their father.

"Wait a minute," I heard him say.

"Did *she* know?" I asked my aunt. "My mother?"

"Yes."

"So why, *why* did she stay with him?"

"Sometimes you take risks in love."

"And sometimes your world falls apart."

"Sometimes you have to remember the good things."

"Did anything good come of it?"

"I'm looking at it now." She sniffed. "We better let those kids in before they explode. Want a tissue?"

I've returned to Dublin a day earlier than planned. I pick up a bottle of wine at the Spar near Trinity College, and an aerosol can of cream just in case. Oh, and a bunch of flowers. I don't know why. Maybe I'll give them to someone.

The hotel I stayed at before has a vacancy. My Armani's hanging in the closet. In the mirror, my scalp is shiny smooth. My leather pants squeak when I twist to check the sides of my head.

The air is bright and fresh as I head off to The George.

It doesn't take long to find him.

I like the way he moves.

I like the ebony of his skin.

I like the warmth of his eyes.

Maybe it's time to take a risk in love.

Maybe I'll e-mail Anton, and request some more leave after London.

0.6% of Sudden Deaths

Sex, I'm told, has many physical and psychological benefits. It boosts the immune system, regulates high blood pressure and helps you sleep well. There is a downside though. People can die during, or soon after sex. It happens more often than you might think. Apparently, up to 0.6% of sudden deaths occur around intercourse. Sex-death is usually linked to heart attacks, and typically happens to middle-aged men, middle-aged men like Ham.

Thankfully, Ham was fucking another man when he carked, not me. But I was there. Well, I might as well have been, because Ham's body was still warm, coated in a thin sheen of sweat when I entered the hotel room.

I hadn't knocked, because he'd been expecting me. Strangely, considering what had just happened, the door was unlocked.

His previous 'guest' was still there, pacing between the grime-smeared window and the bed, as if attempting to shred the already worn-out carpet. He kept whispering, *Oh fuck!* over and over.

Ham was lying on the bed, his eyes and mouth open, tongue lolling out to the side.

I recognised the other guy. We'd shagged in the same hotel a few weeks earlier, though we'd been in a room on the floor above. He was slight, young, with bluish-black skin, and was wearing nothing but a neoprene jock strap. A bottle of lube lay on the floor, oozing its contents onto the already sticky carpet.

"What are we going to do, Zeb?" he asked.

How had this become a 'we' situation?

I'd been expecting a rollicking time with Ham. Instead, I felt like a detective in a murder investigation. Remembering how timid the blue-skinned boy was – the man had literally shook with anticipation when I'd started to fuck him – I took control.

"We haven't done anything wrong." I placed my hand on his shoulder. He flinched. "We need help." Since I was fully dressed, I offered to venture to reception and have a quiet word. "Just give me a minute to figure out what to say." I instructed Blue-skin to make Ham look decent, out of respect. "Perhaps you could start by closing his eyes, and covering his – you know." The situation had made me strangely coy.

"I'm not touching him," the boy said, which struck me as odd, since they clearly *had* been touching each other before I arrived. He sat on the cracked vinyl chair, looking dejected. The seat squeaked as he rocked his neoprene-covered bum back and forth, weeping silently.

Several hours later, a plain white van drove away from the back entrance of the hotel. I'd expected them to stretcher Ham into an ambulance or hearse, not something that looked like a butcher's van.

It was late, and I needed to head home. Otto would be wondering where I was, so I texted my husband, said I'd bumped into a friend who was upset. Otto was a sympathetic man. He'd understand. I needed to comfort the friend, I said, but wouldn't be much longer. The experience of holding the blue-skinned boy as he wept would help me embellish my story with realistic details; only I'd miss out the part where I'd got a stiffy when I massaged his shoulders.

I took the bus home, kept my wide-brimmed hat and sunglasses on, even in the bus's dark interior. I didn't want anyone to recognise me. Two stops away from my destination, I started to feel sad.

I'd known Ham for years. You could say we were friends as well as the other. We were close enough for me to visit him at home. Often, he'd suggest we go out for a ride.

"I'd rather ride you," I remember saying the night he tried to kill me.

Throwing me a helmet, he'd said, "Live a little, Zeb." He talked about six-speed manual gearing and an eighteen sixty-eight cc petrol engine as we stepped into the garage. The figures meant nothing to me, though I had to admit the sleek black bike with its chrome trim was nicely designed. I just wished I didn't have to go anywhere near it.

The sky was darkening as we wove into the traffic. I asked Ham where we were going, but he didn't hear me over the throaty roar of the engine. When we turned left at the next junction though, and left again soon after that, I knew where we were going.

Ham steered the bike onto the motorway like a stunt driver, in and out, left and right, between cars and trucks and other bikes. We passed them on the right. We passed them on the left. I slipped my arms around Ham's waist, as if holding onto him would make a difference. If we collided with one of the articulated lorries he insisted on overtaking, even when they were overtaking someone else, we'd die.

We came within a metre of hitting one, I swear.

I wanted to scream, but dug my nails into the leather of Ham's jacket instead.

I think I'd heard him laugh then, though it was hard to tell with the helmets, the sound of the traffic, and the drum-like beat of my heart.

The bus ground to a halt, and I stepped into the chill night air. There was another k or so to walk to our house. I rubbed my eyes as if that would erase the tears I'd shed for Ham.

Otto didn't normally rise to greet me when I came home late. It wasn't resentment. He was simply a sedentary beast who preferred to remain seated watching pimple-popping videos on YouTube or whatever he was into at the time.

But the night Ham died, he came to the door and held me.

Not a word passed between us.

He held me and let me cry.

Sometimes I think Otto knows more than he lets on.

But if he did, what would be the fun in that?

The M Word

"No." Ronan glanced at the curtain. The light fabric was dancing in a breeze. "Things are fine as they are."

The low light brought dust motes to life and turned the down on his skin golden. He pulled his legs towards his chest and the quilt fell to the floor.

"We've waited so long," I said.

Ronan flicked an invisible speck from his knee, something he did when stressed.

"Why now?" he asked.

"They can't tell us what to do anymore."

"So *you're* telling me what to do instead." He rubbed his knee and flicked again, as if casting away a demon.

"It's what you want too." I stroked his arm. His skin was cool and clammy, despite the heat. "It'll redefine us. Make us clean."

"How do you know what I want?"

"You might not be sure now." I hated the whine of my voice, but continued. "But one day you'll know I'm right." I felt like a sixteen-year-old, rather than a woman in her prime. I was coming across as a sycophant, rather than a lover. I sounded like a kid, rather than an adult, a mother – the mother of someone we both loved. I sounded like a loser not a respected schoolteacher – except

I wasn't a schoolteacher anymore, not since events had caught up with me. Caught me out.

"Maybe one day." He rubbed my ankle with his foot. "Why the hurry?"

Naturally, an average eighteen-year-old wouldn't rush into marriage. But Ronan wasn't typical for his age. He wasn't like the teenagers I'd taught. He was different from my own son. Kyle had also turned eighteen a few weeks earlier. I wondered whether I'd see my child when he transitioned into adulthood, then flushed the thought away. It hurt too much.

My Ronan wasn't a child. He was a man. He worked hard, used his limbs to build the future. His school days were over. His shoulders were broadening, arms like the branches of a mature tree. He wasn't a sapling anymore.

"You'll want a solid foundation. Security."

I was bargaining, negotiating. Not begging.

"And how would becoming your husband help that?"

I didn't have anything left to lose, nothing more I could give, beyond what I already had. I couldn't provide him with an answer, so I asked a question instead.

"Don't you want to make a statement after everything we've been through?" Surely he wanted to fight after years of everyone telling us we were wrong – years of people saying our love was unnatural. This was a way of showing those people they were the ones who were wrong, not us.

"Who would we be making a statement for, Madeleine?" Ronan twisted over, looked me in the eye.

"Us," I said. "You and me."

"But statements aren't for yourselves. They're for other people. Do you think Mum would give a shit whether we were married or not? Would it make everything all right? Would your old school welcome you back into the classroom?"

"It's not about that. It's what I want. For us." My voice was hoarse, barely a whisper. "I thought you'd want it too after everything that's happened. We can be together forever now. No one can stop us." He touched my shoulder, ran a finger down my body, but didn't say anything.

The early evening light was turning the walls amber. We'd leave the bed again soon. Perhaps I'd open a bottle of wine. Maybe we'd have something to eat. Then my man-child would fall asleep and I'd watch him breathe. In. Out. In. Out.

Ronan's work exhausted him, but that wasn't why he rushed to the bedroom when he came home. He needed me – my hands on his back, my lips on his neck.

How long was it since we'd first spent the whole night together? Nearly two years? I'd booked us into a hotel and savoured the sour sweetness of his skin when I woke. We had a whole night together without fear of discovery.

Ronan had been sixteen.

No one could criticise me for taking advantage of him anymore.

We could be together every night for the rest of our lives.

No more sneaking around.

I'd sacrificed so much for this.

My life had imploded when people found out about us. Ronan had been painted as victim, and I was labelled a paedophile. We lost those closest to us. His mother Jacqui had been my friend. And Kyle. My son didn't understand. Ronan had been *his* friend.

This is fucked up, Mum.

How could you?

There's a word for people like you.

There was more. It ended with *I hate you.* I hadn't seen my son for over a year.

Ronan slid out of bed.

"So?" I asked.

"What?"

"Shall we do it?"

"Do what?"

"Will you marry me?"

"We've got this. We don't need anything else." He picked up his guitar, sat on the armchair and strummed some chords, the same ones he always played. He used to be an adept musician. Had I robbed him of that as well?

The late sun inched its way down, dipping towards the horizon. Sweat trickled down my back.

"Come back to bed."

Ronan cast the guitar aside, flicked his knee again as if shooing away a demon. I knew what the demon was. I knew what would happen if the demon pushed Ronan further. He'd squash it. I knew he'd discard the demon if it tried to ensnare him. Yet I knew the demon was persistent.

"We don't have to get married here. We could go somewhere nobody knows us."

"A non-public public statement?" He sneered at me and walked out of the room.

He'd be back. He always came back.

A door banged. I heard the stomp of Ronan's boots on the path, a crunch of gravel, the gate closing.

If he was coming back, it wouldn't be any time soon.

Balloon Phobia and God

I found God through a property manager in North Christchurch. The Almighty sat on the floor of a flat I was viewing in London Street. He was flicking through a copy of *Hustler,* smoking a mentholated cigarette, casually dropping ash onto the carpet.

I was looking for somewhere to live. He was looking at the beauty of human flesh.

I'd been discharged from the military a month earlier, and things were tough. I needed a flat. I needed a job. I needed to get my life on track.

I came home to discover my fiancée Beth no longer saw me as suitable marriage material. She'd left me for a loss-adjuster with a ponytail, said I didn't have the courage of my convictions, whatever that meant. I reckon the loss-adjustor had a better bank balance, or a better arse. Whatever. I was out of the picture.

Renée Morgan was waiting for me outside the flat on a cool Friday evening. I followed the property manager up the external stairs leading to the first floor apartment. Her dagger-heels made a *plink plink* sound. My army boots rang on the treads, like nails hammering tin. I thought her shoes might poke through the gaps in the steps and send her arse over tit. But they didn't.

Renée was well turned out, except for a few wiry hairs poking from her chin. She twisted the key in the door, let the light in ahead of us, and that's when I saw God. Renée acted like she didn't see Him, though she coughed and waved a hand in front of her nose. Guess the cigarette smoke bothered her.

The property manager walked me into the bedroom without a word. I suppose she hoped I wouldn't notice the water stains on the wallpaper, the threadbare carpet, and the pile of crumpled newspapers in the corner. Or the deity sitting on the lounge floor.

None of that put me off. I could move out of Mum's house, where I'd trod uneasily around my stepfather since my return. I had nowhere else to go.

"I'll take it," I said, and Renée launched into discussing bonds and references. She doled the information out quickly, glossing over my details. I guess the landlord wasn't particular about who rented the place.

On Monday, I unloaded cartons of utensils, bin-liners full of clothes, and rickety furniture from the back of my brother-in-law-not-to-be Jason's van. We were still on good terms. He lifted my belongings and dumped them on the pavement outside the flat.

A procession of limousines pulled out of the funeral director's opposite. I took my cap off and bowed my head as the first drops of rain pocked the pavement. Jason shuffled next to me, bags in his arms. He stepped towards the van and back again, before lowering his head too.

Then I looked up at the flat window, in case the Lord had put in an appearance again. He might have wanted to wish the dearly beloved well as they accompanied their loved one's remains to the Linwood cemetery.

When the funeral party departed, Jason shovelled the rest of my things out of his van, whilst I waltzed my mother's easy chair towards the metal steps.

"Well, that'll be it then?" Jason asked when the van was empty. It was a statement and a question at the same time. I didn't know if I was supposed to answer or not, so I didn't. The rain thickened, and I asked a question instead.

"Is he any good for her?"

"Who? Good for what?" Jason seemed in a hurry to get off.

"The loss adjuster with the cute arse. For Beth."

"Phil? He's a good egg. I'd best be goin'." Jason rubbed his gloved hands together against the cold wet air.

"I'd ask you in for a coffee, to say thanks and that, but I'm — "

"Nah, s'allright. I'd best be goin'." Jason hoisted himself up into the driver's cab and roared away.

Another hearse pulled into the funeral parlour. Organ music competed with the random beat of rain on the pavement. I suppose I'd eventually get used to the noisy neighbours.

I grabbed two bags of bedding and bolted up to the flat, two steps at a time. The key stuck in the lock. Had it done that for Renée Morgan? Had it hell.

I leaned against the door, twisted until something clicked, and I was in. A floorboard creaked and my heart thumped in its cage.

"God?"

Silence.

"Almighty one? Father?" I sounded stupid, but there was no one else to hear me, or was there? I wandered from room to room. A minty aroma hung around the place. It competed with the mustiness from the long unopened cupboards.

"You here?"

There was no reply. Bolts of rain hammered against the window like bullets so I ran down to the pavement to pick up the rest of my gear before it got soaked. Two sullen boys in shorts splashed a tennis ball in the gutter. They leered at me with blank questioning looks.

Upstairs, I found tea bags and filled the jug. The tap hissed like an angry cat, and spat out as much air as water. I shuddered. I'm not good with air in places it shouldn't be. It's even worse since I returned from Besmaya. I found two cream-coloured mugs Beth had detested and dropped a teabag in each. One for God and one for me. I wondered if a biscuit might be in order, but couldn't remember where I'd packed the Mallow Puffs.

Stepping out of the kitchen, I tried a new tack.

"Our Father?"

Maybe a prayer was needed. He wasn't in the laundry.

"Who art in − in heaven − "

But was He in heaven?

Probably not, since I'd seen Him clear as a lamppost, sitting cross-legged on the floor last Friday, smoking a fag.

Of course, when Renée showed me the apartment, it wasn't the first time I'd seen God. I'd known Him as a kid.

My stepfather Donald was a mean fucker. He scared the pants off me, knew exactly what frightened me, but acted innocent if anyone caught him tormenting me. Donald discovered my fear of balloons. I don't know how, but he *knew.*

The day before my sixth birthday, Donald turns up with a gigantic black plastic bag. Something's squeaking inside. He waits till it's just the two of us in the lounge, and splits the bag open. Out spill balloons, thirty, forty, a hundred. I don't know.

I scream.

Donald puts his hand over my mouth.

This is fun, *he says, with menace in his voice.*

He holds me close with his other arm. I kick and squirm, tensing like a spring every time one of the – the things brushes past my leg. I'm terrified one's going to go bang.

Where is my mother?

I scream again, but all that comes out is a strangled hoot, like a car horn, as I force the air from my lungs into Donald's cupped hand. He loops an arm around my torso. I'm small for my age, helpless as he lifts me from the ground. He swings my legs through a sea of floating balloons. They bounce like gas-filled severed heads. My stifled screams fill the room like the screech of a harmonica.

And still there's no sign of my mother.

Then I lose control. There's a thud as Donald drops me onto the floor, and the sting of his slap cuts into my face.

You disgusting little shit, *he shouts.*

Mum walks in with a tea towel in her hands. I hang my head in shame as what's left in my bladder trickles through my track pants onto the carpet. Hiss. A green balloon drifts towards me.

Donald points to a dark oval patch on his trousers.

And my mother laughs. She laughs.

That night I wish so hard for God to come and take me away. I squeeze my eyes tight until all the light left in them turns into swirling patterns and window shapes. I hope, and then hope again. He feels so close. I'm sure I see Him, with a full beard, and chalk-white skin.

At least I *think* I saw Him.

God's come to me several times since then. Sometimes He's a pattern in the sky. Sometimes He's there when the other guys get hurt, but we don't. Sometimes He's good weather. Sometimes He's just a feeling.

But when I saw God sitting on the floor of my flat in patched jeans with mud at the knees, I knew He was the real deal. Incarnate. That's what they used to say at Sunday school. God made flesh.

I sipped my tea and looked at the rain-spattered bags waiting to be unpacked. I was investigating a mouldy lemon in the fridge, when God walked into the kitchen unzipping His polar-fleece.

"Got any cigarettes?" He slumped onto a crate of saucepans for want of anything else to sit on.

"Ah, there you are. Wait a sec." I rummaged in a box and found ginger nuts in a zip-lock bag. "D'you wanna biscuit with your tea?" The drink slopped onto the lino by His feet. I made sure the trapped air in the bag didn't do anything unpredictable when I popped it open.

"Nah mate. Just a fag'll do."

"I'll get my ciggies, your − you − anyway, what do I call you?" I grabbed my jacket that was hanging on a peg on the door.

"Terry."

"Terry?" I turned around and looked at Him. "Is that short for something? As in Almighty and Terri − "

"Terence. Like any other Terry. Now where's them durries?"

So, God *did* have a name, and it wasn't Harold. He dragged His sleeve across His nose and snorted. A line of silver mucus streaked onto the blue fabric of His jacket. It was almost beautiful in the grey afternoon light. Divine.

"Here we are." I tipped the last two cigs out of my pack, and passed one to God, a holy offering.

"I prefer mentholated," He said, "but these'll do."

Later, when the rain cleared, we popped out for more cigarettes. We stopped at the Richmond playground. God kicked a ball against the blue mural, that bloody awful mural. Funny, He didn't have a ball with Him when we left the apartment. Guess He must have found it lying around. Or something. The mud and turf churned up under His boots. I dodged over to the side as the black and white ball hurtled towards me.

"Missed!" Honestly, He was like a big kid. Strands of grey-black hair bobbed on His head like spaghetti as He ran past me. "Come on!"

"I'm not good at ball games," I said, heading past a derelict lot towards the dairy. I didn't tell Him why I wouldn't go near the damn ball. Compressed air. Fuck. He must've known though. God knows everything, doesn't He?

"Boring," He sang, and came into step beside me. The ball had disappeared.

We picked up some beers. Or I should say *I* picked up a six-pack. He pointed at the cigarette dispenser. When I asked if He wanted to go halves, He turned the pocket of His polar fleece inside out. Two ten-cent pieces fell out and rolled underneath the counter.

"I'm like the Queen of England," He said, smiling to reveal a broad gap between His front teeth. "I don't carry much cash."

"It's alright, *Terry*," I said. "I'll get these. You get the next lot." I made sure to use *Terry* when we were in public. It wouldn't do to call Him 'our father' to his face whilst the Asian shop dude put my Speight's Gold Medal in a bag.

Back in the flat, we had a laugh once I got the telly working.

My Kitchen Rules, He'd insisted. The programme made us hungry, so I warmed beans in a pan. God didn't eat much. He asked if there was more beer.

"Nah, this is the last one," I said, nudging my toe against the half empty can on the floor.

"Watch this." He grabbed the creamy-beige mugs, swiped my tinny, and blew across the hole on top, and filled both mugs to the brim.

We nattered about all sorts. Hours went by, drinking, drinking, drinking. He poured out more beer. And more.

My eyelids started to close mid-sentence. I was rat-arsed, but tired.

"You'll be arright on the couch?" I asked. "Ah'd besh be off t'bed. Holler if ya need anything – " I headed to the bathroom for a leak.

"Haff anuther beer," was all He said, before tipping more amber fluid into my mug.

And that's the last thing I remember from the first night I hung out with God.

I woke up freezing cold on the lounge floor.

"God?"

No answer.

"Uh – Terry?"

Zilch.

It was still dark, so I flicked the light on. Beer cans lay scattered on the floor. I kicked them into the pile of newspapers in the corner. I peered into the bedroom. Nothing. I pulled the quilt out of its plastic bag, enveloped myself in its scanty fluffiness, and wriggled onto the mattress. It was perishing. I lay for hours, drifting in and out of sleep, my head pounding. *The report of gunfire, the weight of my helmet, the security forces, curling hashish smoke, bodies in the street. The bodies in the street. The explosions. Would those goddamn explosions ever stop?*

When I woke up, God was sitting at the foot of my bed.

My throat was hangover dry. "Jesus Christ!" I tried to swallow the words back. No one wants to be reminded of a dead son, do they? "I mean, sorry. How much did we drink, *Terry*?" I did a beany fart, and wondered how it changed the composition of the air around us.

"Can't you take your liquor?" He asked, inching away from me. He was still wearing the dusty blue polar fleece.

"S'just I thought we only had six tins – "

"Yeah, right." His sarcasm was acidic for the time of day. He pulled a cig from my packet, lit up and sucked hard.

"What shall we do today?" He poked me beneath my left armpit. I stifled a giggle because it tickled.

What was there to do? I could send off job applications, if I could find any vacancies I was qualified for. I could have a go at reading the self-help book from my psychologist, but the words usually danced on the page and hid their meaning. I could carry on unpacking and tidy the flat. Or I could hang out with God.

"Hey cool. DVDs?" He was thumbing through my collection, still in the box, waiting to be unpacked. A long line of ash drooped and threatened to fall onto the carpet.

"Wanna watch *Star Wars*?"

So that's what we did. It was grey and gloomy outside, and we spent the day watching film after film.

Later God popped out and came back with a parcel of fish'n'chips. Guess He must have found His wallet.

"Manna from Heaven," He said, tipping steaming food onto two plates I'd prized from a box on the kitchen floor. He chucked the chip paper, fat and all, into the pile of crap in the corner, and popped the cap off a Steinlager bottle. "Here," He said, passing me the bottle before opening another for Himself. "Got any ketchup?"

"What's it like being You?" I asked, squeezing sauce I'd found in the fridge onto our plates.

"What about it?"

"You know. Knowing all there is to know, being all-powerful, creating *everything*, and − and − whatever else it is you do. What's it like?"

"S'allright," He said picking a strand of hoki from between His teeth.

"Is that it?"

"Yeah. Let's go to the pub after. Whad'ya reckon, Pomeroy's?"

"Okay." I stuffed a chip in my mouth, wiped my finger through the puddle of sauce and licked it. He was on His feet, pulling the blue fleecy jacket on, scratching at yellowy strands in His beard. We drained our Steinlagers, locked up and thumped down the stairs, God's holy boots clanging on the metal treads, mine ringing out behind Him.

It went on like that for months. I couldn't find work. Well I wasn't really looking. Every day, God and I would do something together. Hang around in the park. Walk into town on a Saturday night to look at girls pouring from the clubs. We'd watch movies, or talk about rugby. The weather grew colder. A howling wind blew through the loose windowpanes.

The mess in the flat grew deeper. Anything I hadn't unpacked after a month, stayed in boxes towering to head height in the spare room.

I heard noises from the boxes. Once I saw a little grey body dart between a carton of car magazines and the bag of clothes.

"Think I need some bait," I said as God walked out of the bathroom, my All Blacks towel tied around His waist.

"What for?"

"I've got mice."

"Nah, don't bother."

I got it. They were His creatures. So I left them to it. Left them to nibble at my comic collection, the wires of my speakers that I'd not got round to setting up, the kite Beth had given me for my thirtieth. I left them to gnaw through Mum's photo albums, and her Nottingham lace tablecloth that I'd had to sneak out from under Donald's daughter's noses when Mum died. I left the mice to bite through old birthday cards with my Dad's shaky writing on them. I let the mice turn everything to dust, leaving pellets of poo in their wake.

I came home from a jobseeker support interview one day to discover Him leaping about like a giant kid, hopping between the piles of rubbish. He was blowing bubbles, dipping a plastic wand into a tub. I walked straight out the door again.

Bubbles.

Ew.

I was going to have to have a word with Him about that. That and other things.

The secondhand washing machine I'd bought died, after spewing its soapy contents all over the laundry floor whilst God and I were out at the Casino one night. I worked with my mop and bucket, trying to soak up whatever I could.

"Don't think it'll make any difference."

"Huh?"

"Just leave it," God said.

"But it's tracking into the spare room."

"Ev'rything in there's fucked anyway." He cleared His throat and hawked a greenie into a flyer advertising cut-price heaters, rolled it into a ball and chucked it into the corner of the lounge with all the other rubbish. I couldn't remember the last time either of us had taken out the trash. The mound of junk was edging up towards the ceiling. Fag ends filled old baked bean tins to the brim.

The place was a tip.

And what did my roomie do? He found some scissors buried somewhere in the box mountain, and was paring His toenails, long and curling, flicking them into the pile of mess.

"You know, you could do a bit more to help around the place," I said, my voice squeaky with emotion. Lately I struggled with confrontation.

"Yeah." He shrugged, and carried on separating the yellow talons from His feet.

"And you could help me with the rent too," I hadn't wanted to bring it up, but it needed to be said. "How long have you been here now anyway? Three months? Four?"

"Yeah." He chucked the scissors on the ground, and took a swig from the bright green tin of 'V' next to him.

"Well?"

"Well what?"

"Are you gonna help out?"

"We'll see. Anyway. I'm going to the pub."

I'm going to the pub. For months it had been *we* and *us*. For months, God and I had done everything together. *Let Him,* I thought. *He'll soon come crawling back.*

But He didn't. He didn't come back that night. He didn't come back the next night, or the one after that.

I started to clear out the mess. I got some Chux super-wipes, air freshener, bleach, and rolls of bin bags. I asked Jason to help.

"Sure, mate," he said, "but it'll cost ya."

"Oh?"

"You know, at the dump, they weigh your van before and after, charge you by the ton. Won't be cheap." He cleared his throat. "And there's petrol."

"I ain't got much cash."

"Well – I know a way we can make it cheaper."

That's how I found myself on Dyer's Pass Road in the middle of the night, chucking my shit out of Jason's van. We tipped it over the bluff, careful not to lose our footing. We had to work fast. Anyone might see us and call the cops.

Afterwards, Jason and I headed back to London Street.

"So, how is she then?"

"Eh?" Jason coaxed the van into a lower gear as we turned the corner. There were lights on at the funeral parlour. Shadowy figures moved within the windows. I'd never seen anyone in there at night before. Jason pulled the handbrake up outside the flat. It was nearly three o'clock in the morning. I didn't get out of the van straight away. I wanted to chat, even though the pong of mould, and all the other crap that had oozed out of my bags was overpowering.

"Beth. How is she?"

"She's good."

"And, she still with ponytail-man?"

"Phil? Yeah."

Something churned in the pit of my belly. I hadn't thought about Beth much in the last few months. Not like I used to, every day, every hour of every day. I'd been too busy doing things with God.

"And you?" Jason asked. "How you doin'?"

"I found God."

"Oh?" There was an edge to his voice, something between pity and disapproval. "No, that's good, I mean it's great," he continued.

"Yeah, but I think I just lost Him again."

"Oh," Jason said, his tone neutral. "Well, I'd best be goin'. Cheers for the petrol money."

I let myself out of the van, and climbed up the stairs, fiddled with the key, in-out-in-out, until the door popped open. I flicked the lights on. The smell of stale cigarettes and wet stuff hit my nostrils, but the lounge was bright and clear. I popped my head into the spare bedroom. The stained carpet was dotted with the few boxes and bags I'd held onto. I looked into the bathroom, the laundry, and my bedroom. Zilch.

"Terry?" I said weakly, just in case there was somewhere I *hadn't* checked. "God?"

Nothing.

I found a saucer to use as an ashtray, and lit a fag. It was the first time in ages I'd bought normal cigarettes, not mentholated.

I kicked my boots off and crawled into bed. It was a warm night, but I shivered.

I was drifting off to sleep, when I heard a bang. A bomb. A fucking bomb in Christchurch. I sat up, my teeth rattling. Then there was another. Bang. Pop. Bang-a-Bang.

What the fuck?

I snuck into the lounge, and there He was, grinning like a maniac. The room was full of balloons. Grey streaks of dawn-light fingered the sky outside, silhouetting Terry's dancing limbs.

"I got these." He tipped more out of a black plastic bag. "Thought they'd brighten the place up." I suppressed the urge to scream. He stirred His hands through the floating balloons, took one and rubbed it on His polar fleece, and then gently stuck it to the wall. I couldn't move.

"That's cool innit?" He picked up another, a green one, rubbed it on His fleece and came towards me.

"FUCK OFF."

"Eh?" He jumped from one foot to the other, almost tripped over a cluster of yellow and mauve balloons.

"I hate them. I hate balloons. You should *know* that."

"What? How can anyone hate balloons?" He pushed the green balloon against my chest. I came close to throwing up. "I brought them home to celebrate."

"*Home?* You don't even live here. Why don't you just fuck off?"

"Mate. You don't mean that, mate."

"Get those things out of here."

"Aawl right." He started popping the balloons, with His feet, with His hands, even His teeth. It was horrible. I rushed into the bedroom and sat on the floor, fingers in my ears, shaking.

The banging stopped, and there was a gentle tap on the door.

"Mate?"

I swung it open in His face.

"You're not really God are you?" My voice was calm, controlled.

"God?" He smiled at me, arms akimbo. "You get some funny ideas into that head of yours sometimes, mate." The carpet was littered with the dead skins of balloons. There were three intact ones in the corner, red, yellow and green.

"Get. Rid. Of. Those. Things. NOW." I felt like crying.

"Okay mate, calm down."

Terry led me by the arm into my bedroom, closed the door. I sat on the edge of the bed, breathing heavily.

"I thought you'd be pleased." He nudged me with his elbow. "Thought you'd be happy to see me."

I was, but I couldn't tell him that. I said nothing.

"Don't you want to know what the surprise is, what we're celebrating?"

"What?"

"I got us somewhere new to live."

"What'd'ya mean?"

"Well, we can't stay here anymore, so I got us a place in a squat. You'll love it. Real fancy, really – "

"What do you mean, *we can't stay here anymore?*"

"These came. They're from her with the heels and facial hair."

He took a pile of letters out of the pocket of his polar fleece, six of them. I pulled them from their envelopes, waited until the words stopped dancing, and read them. They were from Renée Morgan, outlining the process of my eviction.

"You bastard." I threw the letters on the floor, pushed his chest. Hard. I walked out of the bedroom, skirted around a few intact balloons and ran out of the door. At the top of the metal steps, I lit a cigarette, drew in the smoke. I wasn't sure if I was angrier with Terry, or with myself for being such a shmuck.

"Mate." The front door opened a crack. "Hey. Have you calmed down?" He stepped out and stood next to me, leaning against the railings. "Give us a fag."

"You're a fucking freeloader. Get the fuck out of my hair right now."

"Hey but – "

"I mean it. Stay away from me." I edged away from him.

"Aw but – "

That's when everything went mental. I grabbed him by the scruff of the neck, pulled him towards me.

"Get, the, fuck, out of my life." I thought one of the neighbours might come out to see what the noise was about. No one did. It was still early.

"We can work something – "

I squeezed the rest of his words into silence as I tightened the grip around his throat. He kicked my shin. I punched him with my free hand. He put his fingers to his eye, shouting, screaming. I pushed. He pulled. It must only have been a second between him slipping over the barrier, and the crunch-thud of his body landing on the concrete below.

Still no one came.

"Terry?" I looked over the railings. He wasn't moving. A maroon bulb oozed out from the side of his head, wetting the silver-black hair on that side. Shit. It grew larger, fuller, like someone blowing up a balloon. I was frozen to the spot. I clenched and squeezed everything to stop my bladder from emptying. Any minute now, someone would come out and see what had happened. See what I'd done. The reddish-brown circle was the size of his head. Then it stopped growing. My ears were ringing, the silence around me deafening. One by one bangs and crashes broke into the silence.

Exploding artillery. Batteries of howitzers. The bodies on the streets. The bodies on the streets.

My cigarette was still glowing on the ground. I stubbed it out with my toe, closed my eyes, and opened them again. I edged down the steps, forcing one foot in front of the other. *The bodies on the streets.* I held onto the railing, closed my eyes again at the bottom.

I twisted round and opened my eyes.

Terry had gone.

I ran to the spot where I'd seen the red circle. I sank to my knees, brushed my hands against the concrete, and examined them for blood. For stigmata.

Something was banging between my ears. *Boom-thud-boom-thud-boom-thud.* I thought about the bodies in the street. The explosions.

"Terry!" I shouted. Loud. "Where are you, you sly bastard?" Someone opened a door. "I know you're there," I continued. A neighbour came out of her flat. Someone I never spoke to, an old Pakistani woman with a drooping eyelid.

"Ebhritheeng ol right?" She twisted her scarf around her neck. I tried not to stare at the hairs growing from the mole above her eyebrow.

"Yes, we're fine," I said. "*I'm* fine."

"I hear the shouting."

"It's nothing."

I lit another cig and paced towards the Richmond playground. With each step, the banging in my head grew louder. Stronger. More frequent, until the gaps between the explosions all but disappeared.

I walked on, looked over my shoulder, in case.

But there was no sign of Terry.

Just that god-awful banging.

That banging's in my head again.

Feels like my ears are going to burst.

It's the banging that never stops.

And I wish to god that it would, just for a minute.

The Gift

I'm going to buy Otto a present.

It can't be anything expensive. I don't have much cash to spare. Generally, I decide how many shifts I work, and recently I've chosen not to take on too many. Let's just say I've been doing other things. My pay packet reflects my choices.

There's a food dehydrator at *GoodDeals*. It's on sale for $119.96, reduced from $199.95, and I reckon it's exactly what my husband wants.

I missed our anniversary, but Otto has always appreciated the gifts I give him for no reason. Given he's not a very spontaneous person, I find this amusing.

Only there *is* a reason I want to give Otto something today.

I think I'm falling in love with someone else.

I'm falling for a boy with blue–black skin.

I've been meeting Johan twice, three, sometimes four times a week. He brings me flowers. They're not something every gay man appreciates, and not something I can take home too often without questions being asked. Someone Johan met when he lived in Ireland used to give him flowers, and he's loved them ever since.

We leave bunches in water jugs in the hotel rooms where we fuck, and hope the cleaning staff will take them home and enjoy the orange blooms. He usually brings me orange, though recently he's added yellow to the mix.

Otto and I had a dehydrator, but it's broken. Like many of our contraptions that have stopped working, we keep it, in case one day we might find someone who can repair the thing. That day hasn't yet come to pass.

Some things are harder to fix than others.

There are jars of dried lemon, kiwi fruit, apple chips and candied kumquats in our larder. They sit alongside bottles of marmalade Otto made when we were given bagsful of Seville oranges.

The dehydrated strawberries went a long time ago, but isn't that always the way with the best things?

Johan says I should leave my husband. He wants me to start a new life with him, and though I love him when I'm with him, I don't think that's what I want. It's not just Otto. I've been seeing Mervin too, and there are things I do with Mervin I've never done with anyone. It would be too difficult to give him up, and that is what Johan wants. He wants me all to himself.

"It's not that easy," I tell him, as I lay marigold petals on his body, and then lick them off his skin, nibbling each petal before I swallow. "For one thing, I'm married. There's a lot that would have to be undone."

"Then undo them, Zeb. For me." He kisses my back, one vertebra at a time, and inserts a finger into me. "I don't want to share you."

Sometimes Johan is so gentle it makes me want to scream.

It can take up to forty-eight hours to dry food in a dehydrator. The model I'm looking at has a bottom-mounted fan and heating element to ensure consistent airflow for optimum drying. There are six shelves. Although it's a present for Otto, like many things I buy for my husband, it's for me as well. I want to try pineapple. I've never done pineapple before. Did you know it's possible to dry yoghurt in a dehydrator too?

I found Johan on *Splodge.org*. He says he found me. The truth lies somewhere in between. I suppose we found each other.

I use my best profile photo on that site. In fact, though I've registered on a couple of others, I hardly use them anymore. *Splodge* always yields the best results. Mervin is proof of that.

The best fruit leather I made included mangoes, plums and nectarines. It's a good idea to add a little lemon juice to the purée, not that you need the acid to preserve the fruit, but it helps brighten the flavour and maintain the colour of the produce.

Usually, it takes twelve hours to make fruit leather in a dehydrator. You can tell when it's ready, as the finished product is no longer sticky to touch.

That summer, someone gave us a bag of nectarines. Otto and I found other fruits at the market. I made several batches. We ate so much, it made us tingle. I gave some away, squeezed what I could into the freezer. Nothing went to waste. Every piece was put to good use.

Johan is a lawyer. He's only been qualified a few years. He plans to specialise in criminal law. Though he has to be careful what he lets me know, Johan tells me stories about the bad boys he represents. He is legally bound to keep some secrets from me, though there are things I do that take him to the brink, and he has broken an occasional rule.

He wears a suit for court, though there are some cases for which he must wear a wig and gown. I've begged him to meet me in his work clothes, but he refuses.

"Those things are murder to clean," he tells me, and I must content myself with him in his exercise gear, though sometimes there is a little surprise underneath.

I used to make beef jerky in our old dehydrator, but there was a time something went wrong. Otto and I both fell sick. He looked after me, making soups and lemon drinks, even though he was ill himself.

~

Sometimes I find it hard to know the difference between right and wrong.

It feels so right when I'm with Johan.

Though I know it's wrong, I never want it to end.

The Love Nest

She walks towards me. For a fraction of a second, I imagine Jacqui's going to embrace me, to comfort me as she used to years ago. She walks faster, and I turn, running away from the house, from her, down the long driveway, back to the gate.

When I look again, she's closing in, though she's having trouble running in her slippers. Her expression has changed. The mother protecting her cubs has become a hunter ready to strike. I dodge behind the macrocarpa hedge at the entrance, daring to peek at her around the corner. Jacqui stops, raises her hand to shield her eyes from the low April sun. She squints. I back further away and dense foliage cuts the view of the drive, the house, of Jacqui. I can't see her anymore, but she can't see me either. By the time she reaches the road, I've slipped into my car and am driving fast. There's an acceleration skid and squeals of rubber blacken the air. The mother-hunter becomes an angry line in my rear-view mirror. I turn left and she disappears from view.

Jacqui was my best friend. She was my rock when I went through hell. She was sister, mother, doctor, clown; counsellor, wise-woman, nurse. Jacqui was all these things to me, but she couldn't give what I needed most:

acceptance. Without that, my relationship with her son Ronan was doomed. Things may still not have worked out if Jacqui had understood, but Ronan and I might have had a chance if we'd had someone on our side. It wasn't our age difference that killed the relationship. It was the isolation, the severing of ties to our old lives.

I ease off the pedal, but my heart is still racing. That was close. Jacqui must have caught a glimpse of me, an intruder, when I stood at the window. My breath frosted the glass as I peered through a gap in the curtains. She came after me before I could take in the details inside, before I could assess how the place had changed since I'd last visited.

The house is beautiful, the sort of home Ronan and I dreamed of when we were together. Apricot light filters through glass domes suspended from the ceiling. The carpets look lush, expensive. Creamy. Impractical.

Ronan's car wasn't there. His wife kept her Mazda in the garage, but he parked his Tesla in front of the arched doorway, even though they had enough garage space to accommodate four cars. There was a familiar car in its place: Jacqui's.

Ronan wasn't home, but I'd still wanted to look inside. I'd pushed my nose against the pane and watched.

Jacqui had passed Gretchen a plastic water bottle. Ronan's wife was dark haired and sickeningly pretty. Her slim legs rested on a footstool. She had a cushion on her knees, and was nursing a dome-headed baby.

That baby was nothing to me. It didn't elicit any emotion. No hatred. No love. No jealousy. No coochee-coochee-coo. It was just an organism feeding from its mother's body. Gretchen's face was etched with emotion though. I remembered that love-intoxicated feeling. I'd felt it with my son Kyle, years ago. Somewhere in the city at the same time, Jacqui will have been feeling it with her own son. But that was before I knew her. Before our boys became best friends. And it was long before I fell in love with Jacqui's son.

Those connections between us are all broken.

Why hadn't I left when I saw Jacqui's car? I knew she was there, yet I'd continued walking beside the gravel pathway, two sheep staring at me lazily as I placed each foot carefully on the grass verge so I didn't make a sound. A pair of dragonflies had flitted in the late afternoon sun like drunken dancers. I knew Jacqui was there, and still I went to the house, drawn like a pin to a magnet.

Had I wanted Jacqui to see me?

Maybe.

I've been to that house before. The first time was before their wedding.

It hadn't been easy to find. Took hours of searching and some deceptive phone calls, to discover the *lifestyle block* my ex-lover had acquired with his fiancée: five bedrooms, garaging for four cars, an orchard and grazing.

A large pond, fenced off for safety.

I'd been to their rental as well, soon after Gretchen moved in.

Also, I'd been to the multi-storey building that housed a suite of offices where Gretchen worked. I'd climbed the steps beside the living wall to the fifth floor and pretended I was lost when the receptionist asked if he could help. I found Gretchen's name on a door as I turned to leave and had wondered whether she planned to keep her surname after they married, or if she'd take Ronan's.

And I was there *that* day.

No one checks latecomers arriving at a church for a wedding. No one asks to look at the invitations. No one notices, especially if the uninvited guest comes dressed in an expensive suit, something they might have worn to their own wedding, if only they had snared the man first. They are ushered to a back seat in silence.

Gretchen was walking down the aisle on her father's arm. I'd struggled to breathe properly. I had to calm myself by counting. One-two-three-hold three-two-one-hold. Gretchen was everything Jacqui could wish for in a daughter-in-law. But was she what *he* wanted?

Ronan is an untamable spirit. I couldn't pin him down.

At least I haven't been able to yet.

Just because he's married, it doesn't mean I never will.

As I park in front of my house, my nosey neighbour Burt Hartley gives me the evils. I smirk at him confident I can overcome anything. It's only a matter of time.

Ronan will be back.

He loves me.

He knows I'm waiting.

Bagdogra Airport

I'm drinking the worst cup of tea I've ever tasted. A pistachio ice cream melts in front of me. I swear there's a fly's wing in it.

"Take it back," Alice says, cupping my hand in hers. I pull away.

I beckon to the waitress, who hitches up her lurid green sari and waddles over like a lettuce on wheels.

I show her the wing. She takes my spoon, scoops the appendage out. The rest of the insect's body follows. The woman wipes the spoon on a green cloth that's tucked into her waist, returns it, looking at me like I'm an incompetent child.

"There," she says only it sounds like *dare.* She walks away.

"Let's get out of here," Alice says. She grabs her backpack, and I follow her into the searing green light that filters through the canopy outside the cafeteria.

Everything is green.

I haven't seen so much green in all the time we've been in India. Apart from the cotton wool snow-peaked Himalayas in the distance, there is green everywhere. The terraced tea plantations, the glint of it in the trees, even the liver-coloured turds in the long-drop toilets are tinged a sappy green.

In the market, a tarpaulin flaps as a hot wind blows through. It offers little protection to the scarves and shawls that sit beneath it like folded butterflies. It stopped raining half an hour ago, and immediately everything was engulfed in a steamy heat. Grey clouds hover in the distance, and water trickles through roadside channels, reminding us things might change at any moment.

"Gen-u-in Dar-ji-ling tea," a boy shouts. He runs between potential targets, tugging at their clothes. He's luring them into the cafeteria Alice and I just left, where they'll be served polystyrene containers of over-stewed cha with obligatory sugar and milk. And flies. The boy nearly runs into me when I stop to light a beedi.

"Chale jao," I order, and he skitters away. I need the toilet.

Alice pushes through a crowd of locals towards a stall displaying a kaleidoscopic array of T-shirts. I follow. Her familiar laughter jars, and that's when the urge I've felt all week grows stronger. She hands the vendor some notes and coins, tosses her head, throwing a halo of dreadlocks into the air, an irritating gesture, but how can you tell someone to stop doing something like that? She pushes her sequined purse back into the pocket of her faded blue jacket. The effort required to manoeuvre her backpack onto her shoulders is a reminder of her condition. I could offer to help, but I don't. She's deep in conversation anyway, likely being persuaded to part with more cash.

A hawker shouts. "Take? You will take? Give good lucks for new Millennium." He pushes a laminated sheet onto my chest. "Two rupee." The sheet has images of Ganesh, Kali and Michael Jackson printed on it. At least it looks like Michael Jackson. I walk away. A tiny girl no higher than my thigh jingles dancing bells at me. Her bare feet splash through puddles. Her tattered frock is several sizes too big, and circles of brown skin poke through the holes.

I place my fingers over my groin to feel the passport bag under my jeans, to check the bag is still there, to push on the satisfying bulk of it. The pressure on my abdomen reminds me I need a slash. The child holds out a set of bells, and smiles. I turn away to see what Alice is doing. She's still talking. Her silhouette against the yellow-green light emphasises her pregnancy. She looks so different these days.

When I met Alice, she was working at the Carrington1 bar. She reached up for the optics, revealing inches of bare belly, taut and tanned. I knew then, that she'd be coming home with me, if not that night, then soon. I wanted to crush her slight body under my own.

Alice is one of those women who become broad rather than curvaceous when pregnant. An old woman in Delhi said it meant she was carrying a boy. I think it makes her look dumpy. Her dreadlocks are matted and fraying. They were sleek and shiny the night we met. She'd handed me a glass and our eyes locked. The buzz and bustle of the Carrington1 had continued around us, but it was as if we were the only ones there.

~

I run my fingers through my dreads. Wish I had the gear to look after them properly. My body is changing. My breasts are sore. I put my fingers to my lips, and there's a musty smell from my scalp. I work hard to suppress the retching and nausea.

Mac's been looking at other girls recently, even some of the locals, wearing little more than a band of fabric around their brown bodies. There was a time when he looked at me like that. Hungrily. I need something to make me feel beautiful again. Something special.

~

This has been a difficult journey. Alice picks over shirts and holds them up to the citrus light. We started travelling six months into our relationship. I was tentative about coming away with her so soon, but I liked the feel of her back curving against my chest in bed, and thought I might miss it.

Now it's turned into a different sort of adventure.

If I'd come on my own, I could have seen more, done more, tried more. I could have disappeared into unknown territory, but there's no point dwelling on that now.

I told Alice I loved her before we came away. The words slipped through my lips at the peak of my orgasm, before I could stop them.

Her sickness started soon after we reached Thailand. She lost weight, and felt tired all the time. Her face puffed up and was covered in spots. We put it down to the change in climate, the water, anything but the obvious.

We carried on travelling.

After she saw the doctor in Delhi she came back to the hotel glowing.

"Look Mac!" She showed me a sonogram. I'd suppressed the fear that crept up my gullet, and forced a smile.

I dip into the side street, look behind me once, and quicken my pace. I untie my ponytail hoping it will release the tension that creeps across my scalp.

About three streets from the market, a crowd pours out from a white building. They're leaving a concert. The women are dressed in colourful silk, a flotilla of turquoise, magenta and lime green. The men wear white linens, which contrast with the leathery brown of their skins. My khaki shirt is conspicuous for its drabness, and offers little camouflage. The crowd thins, and I look back over my shoulder, walk a little faster. There's a hole in my shoe, and my sock is wet. In the distance, the bass boom of a temple gong resonates, and the reek of incense penetrates the air.

I walk toward a line of auto-rickshaws, and signal a driver who's leaning against a post. Squeezing my pack into the cavity of the yellow and turquoise auto, I climb into what is little more than a bloated scooter. The driver hawks a red line of paan-stained spit onto the ground, and mounts his seat. His chest rattles so badly, he should have died years ago. Other rickshaw-wallahs crowd around me offering discounted prices to temples and markets. I hand my guy a wad of rupees, and shout, "Go, go now!" He twists the throttle, and we set off.

"Where you go?"

I tell him my destination. "Can you take me?" He doubles back and heads in the direction we came from. A traveller in a faded blue jacket is negotiating with another driver near the post, and I almost piss myself, I need to go that badly.

"It too far," he says. "I take you to truck stop. You get car there to take you." The driver pulls into a stream of belching lorries. Blue-jacket turns to look at me. I look straight into her — but it's a guy, a guy with missing teeth. I rummage in my pocket for the pack of beedis.

~

When I hold the shirt up to the strange greeny-yellow light, I'm stunned by the intricate embroidery. Swirling zodiac patterns. *Seventeen different threads* the vendor says, eager to make a sale. It's so beautiful. I hand him the cash. I want to wear it now, so I throw my pack on the ground, slump my jacket over it.

"You are liking?" the stallholder says.

"I love it," I tell him.

"Hey Mac, check this out." I stretch the purples, blue and crimson stitches over my abdomen, over our baby. I look around. Mac's wandered off somewhere. "Mac," I shout, struggling to be heard over the din of the market.

Where's he gone?

~

I really need to pee, so when we reach the truck stop, I jump out of the rickshaw without tipping the driver. I probably gave him a week's wages already anyway. It's warmer and drier at the truck stop than it was in town. A bunch of local guys thread in and out of the shacks where you can buy anything from monkey curry to a cheese-burger. It's been hours since I ate, but I have no appetite. I sneak into a gap behind the stalls, pull my cock out and piss into the dusty earth. A small girl creeps out of one of the huts and stares at me. I shake drips off my penis and stare back at her.

It doesn't take long to strike a deal. A guy wearing a Penn State shirt will take me. It's stinking hot in his truck, but I have to wait for him to load packages onto the roof. I hope there's air-con, but there probably won't be.

Maybe I should go back — but no. That would be stupid.

~

It's so hot, but a cold chill racks my body. My new shirt is circled with sweat under the arms. I need to control my breathing, but it's hard, so hard. Did I walk down this alley already? Fuck, I'm back where I started. There's the shop where I — must stop breathing so fast — bad for the baby — where is he? The distance. The distance between us. I didn't imagine it. He's been looking at other girls recently. My breathing. Hungrily. I — I must stop breathing —

breathing so fast. I didn't imagine the distance between us. It's real.

He has all our money.

~

My eyes are dry and sandy. The truck pulls away, and I step into the belly of Bagdogra Airport. It's as warm inside as out. I shrug off my jacket and strap it to my pack. A skinny guy with a canker over his eye mumbles something and tugs at my pack.

"What? No. Leave it."

"I for you carry. I help." He's surprisingly strong for his scrawny build. The man tries to wrest my luggage from me, but I shoo him away, like he's a fly.

"No. No help. I can do it myself."

I buy a fizzy drink and extinguish the furnace in my throat. Then the battle to change my flight begins.

~

I trudge up the hill towards the backpackers we stayed at last night, and god — my pack is so heavy. Someone outside the entrance speaks to me, and my voice cracks when I try to reply. I'm breathing so fast. There's laughter and Western pop music coming from inside the building.

I describe Mac to the receptionist, ask if he's been back.

"No, Madam." The guy smiles and shakes his head from side to side, like a bobblehead doll. "You want a room?"

"I need," I begin, but I have no idea what I need. That's when the tears come.

Mac's been looking at other girls recently.

Shafts of sunlight trace patterns onto the foyer floor. They blur through my teary eyes. The receptionist sits me down behind the counter, and barks an order to a skinny man. Minutes later, he returns with the proprietor. A small boy brings a glass of nimbu-paani on a tray. I sip, because I'm so dry even though I don't like the lemon-water drink everyone seems to serve here.

"You not fly Kolkata today, Madam?"

"Kolkata? No."

"Your husband, he telephone Bagdogra Airport this morning, but line is bad."

My husband? Kolkata?

"I need a taxi. Get me a taxi now." My voice is petulant and strained. I sound like my mother.

But then I remember. I grab my sequined purse, and pull out a roll of notes. A shower of coins falls to the floor. There's barely enough in there for a meal, let alone a taxi. Two ragged children materialise to help pick up the money I dropped. It's only when I start to thank them that they run off with my coins. I'm still breathing really fast, and my hysterical laughter is a rabid animal noise that splits the air. I wipe hot tears with the back of my hand.

The hill was so steep on the way here I had to stop three times.

~

I walk away from the counter scratching my chin. The airport lounge is heaving. There is a low murmur from a hundred conversations. I've been travelling for months and am covered in grime, but still I'm reluctant to drop my luggage to the ground. Brown and grey stains tar the airport floor. The hot human smell in the terminal suggests the airport's army of cleaners fight a losing battle. I pull my knotty hair back into a ponytail.

I'm close to the front of the queue. Time to get my passport out. A tattered photograph falls out. Two smiling faces. I have my arm around Alice. A haggard mother to my right struggles to calm a screaming child. Does Alice know yet?

The mother lays her child on the filth of the airport floor. The wriggling toddler tries to roll away as she begins the ritual of changing its bum. The stink adds to the aroma of stale curry, sweat and cigarette smoke that chokes Bagdogra airport. The toddler smiles at me, and there's a glint of creamy new teeth in its mouth. I look away, and try to stop thinking about the rancid brown mess that is pancaked onto the child's arse. Though I turn away from the nauseating sight, I can't escape the oniony smell. My stomach lurches.

An emaciated woman with a humped back shuffles past. She wears minimal underclothing beneath her holed sari, and brushes over the debris on the floor using an ineffectual jhatta, producing a swirl of dust. A cacophony of blowflies circles the globes that illuminate the lounge. I screw up the photo and toss it into an overflowing litterbin. It misses and bounces onto the blotched white tiles.

~

The woman is from Berlin. I swear I'll pay her back some day, though fuck knows if I ever can. I insist I will though, as I wave through the open window of the taxi. Stupid, as I haven't taken note of her address, and will never be able to find her.

What if I'm making a mistake? Could he have become disorientated? Is Mac still wandering the streets of Darjeeling?

I might be wrong, but I'm probably not. We were heading for Sikkim, not Kolkata.

"What is your destination, Madam?" the taxi driver smiles through paan-stained teeth.

"Bagdogra Airport." I look for a seatbelt, but there isn't one. "Quickly, please."

~

"Calling all passengers ..."

My flight's departure is announced over the Tannoy. My leg jumps, and I suck hard on the stub of my fag. A family dressed in identical tracksuits comments about the places they're planning to visit, until someone behind them interrupts. Accusations fly about stealing places in the queue. I clench my teeth and toy with the boarding pass poking from my worn passport.

On the tarmac, I head towards the metal steps leading to the aircraft. Beside the runway, the green grass is vibrant and exhilarating. Something inside me relaxes, like a long exhalation. I climb into the plane without looking back.

~

When I burst into the departure lounge, my eyes are sore, and my breath comes in short bursts. My backpack is still too heavy, even though I dumped half my stuff in the taxi. I'm not even running, but I'm out of breath.

At the information desk, my tongue fails to articulate. I sound incoherent. A little less like my mother now, a little more like a mad woman. Eventually I tell the clerk what I need to, but she says she can't help me. I bang my fist on the desk. Even if I *had* memorised Mac's passport number, she says, she couldn't do anything for me.

I slump into one of the rigid seats and cradle my head in my hands, tears washing through my fingers. I need a plan. I need a plan, but right now I can't think.

I take the torn and faded photograph from the side section of my sequined purse. Mac's smiling face, so carefree. A protective arm wrapped around me. I look so young, so happy.

Mac's been looking at other girls recently. There was a time when he looked at me like that. Hungrily. I need something to make me feel beautiful again. But I know I'll never find it.

Through the window there is a miniscule dot of a retreating aircraft.

It fades into the distance, beyond my reach.

Success

We're running along Brighton Beach: Kyle and me tugging at our kites.

I took Harry and Ness to see the kites on Brighton Beach yesterday. The council organise an annual kite day: kites soaring, bursting the summer sky. Kites shaped like dolphins, sharks, stingrays, eagles and astronauts. Some were simply kite-shaped, including the crappy one I bought that refused to fly.

Maybe that's why I dreamed about my childhood friend, Kyle. We used to fly kites on this beach. Even the windiest days were glorious, or maybe my memory's flawed. The reality may have been colder, with snotty noses and sand blowing in our eyes.

The kids were bored after ten minutes. They wanted ice cream. Gretchen was working. My wife's firm had taken on too many clients, so they were doing extra hours, even on a Saturday, something to do with the tax year.

Ness's ice cream fell onto the grey sand and she started crying. I took the kids home, washed them, tried to feed them something nutritious, had an aborted game of Monopoly, and then plugged them into a film on television, so I had time to think.

Hana had sent a text.

I need to change my phone settings. Can't have visible incoming messages when I'm juggling two women.

Before I could read what Hana's had said, Gretchen called.

"Did you give Ness two servings of veggies?"

"Is a serving of mashed potato equivalent to a serving of kale?" I snapped. "Does it matter that kale is eighty-five per cent water?" I was sick of her questioning my parental competence. She left me holding the babies so often, why did she think I needed to be told what to do? "What if half a serving fell on the floor?"

"Come on, Ronan. I'm only trying to help. Anyway," she said, "I won't be home till late. Maybe ten. Make sure Harry has a wee before bed."

"You don't need to remind me."

My wife behaves as if she's the only one with responsibilities. She assumes I'm free to have the kids whenever she's busy.

Hana's text was short and to the point. She wanted to see me. I'd tried calling her, but there was no reply.

Sunday night, and I'm left with the kids again.

Gretchen and I had a fight.

I have responsibilities too.

You can work from home. I can't.

Not with these two around.

Ness wants an ice cream, but the ones we have in the freezer won't do. It has to be like the one she had yesterday.

Harry whacks her because he wants to be Batman in their game, not Elsa.

It takes ten minutes to separate the kids without killing them.

I have five unread messages. I'm about to check them when I hear screams. It's time to be firm. Death by toothbrush. They're only milk teeth anyway.

When the kids fall asleep, I tackle six work-related emails.

I'm a successful man, but what have I achieved? Sure, I have the beautiful house and wife. Such a cliché. I hate clichés. The kids will receive the best schooling. Mum was very firm about that. With being a teacher, she knows where we *shouldn't* send them. If we have to pay, we'll pay. We can afford it.

I email a geotech engineer, plug my headphones in, play two pieces of music simultaneously and read Hana's messages.

The double music thing is something I discovered when the company took off. It parallels the chaos in my mind. I can't be CEO of one of the largest construction firms in the city, juggle two wailing children and keep my shit together without exercising my mental agility in some way. I find Scarlatti's sonata in D minor partners well with anything by Scott Joplin, and at a push *The Nutcracker* by Tchaikovsky. Frank Zappa pairs well with Tchaikovsky, but *never* mix The Stones with Vivaldi. They clash.

I read the texts in reverse order.

Talk to me, Ronan, or I'll tell your wife everything.

Oh fuck.

We have to talk.

Ring me.

I want more than this.

Ring me. Please. You know why.

I ring Hana.

Chopin's *Marche Funèbre* thumps unaccompanied. Minnie Riperton's *Lovin' You* has finished, and that music stream has wound to a halt.

Hana doesn't reply. I flick something from my knee, but know there isn't really anything there. It's just a habit I have when mulling over things.

A haunting moan from Ness's bedroom floats through the house. Gretchen would have rushed in, cradled the child and brought her in with us. I ignore Ness. She'll settle on her own. I need to email a quantity surveyor.

Hana, why do you have to complicate things?

We took Hana on as an intern. She was sixteen, all large eyes and long legs. She knew I wanted her, and she played me.

Some guy almost succeeded in taking out a disciplinary after I promoted Hana ahead of five candidates who were frankly five times better than she was. She wouldn't let me fuck her until we'd signed the contract. Bitch.

First she text bombs me, and now she won't answer her freaking phone. Where's she gone? Probably out with her teenage friends, listening to music that oscillates around a single note, sampling fragments of forty-year-old songs.

Hana doesn't *get* my listening to two pieces of music simultaneously. She doesn't have the mental discipline to syncopate the two patterns in her mind. She doesn't understand classical music full stop.

I didn't understand it either when I was her age. Someone taught me to count the sequences, look for patterns. She'd tap rhythms on my bare chest then go down on me.

We hid our forbidden love for years. Is that what I have with Hana? Will it end the same way? I had the classical music lover for years, and then I threw her away.

Maybe *that's* why I dreamed about my childhood friend. It isn't only Kyle and me in that dream. His mother's there too. Scarlatti's *Fandango* plays on her phone held in one hand. There's a kite string clutched in the other, bobbing in stately time to the harpsichord.

Hairs Between My Teeth

If, like me, you have specific preferences when it comes to guys, *Splodge.org* is the best dating app for you. I don't receive any sponsorship from these people, by the way. They simply provide the greatest choices.

If you want gentle m2m, there are sweet individuals on offer. If you want rough and dangerous, your needs will be met, too. Perhaps you're going through an ambiguous phase? There are options on the site's pages to scratch that particular itch.

Want to go large? Look no further. I've also found men with pencil-thin attributes who have other features that make up for what's lacking in the girth department.

Want your man to talk dirty? There's a whole section dedicated to that.

Do you like men with piercings? Although I say so myself, I believe my profile shot on that page is one of the best. It's a still from a movie I made. My tongue rests seductively over my lower lip, a diamond stud flashing against my front teeth.

And what about hair? I've been lucky enough to find unusually hairy beings on the site, tucked in amongst men with smoother bodies. Although that description evokes an appealing visual image, in reality I experienced them one at a time.

Take Mervin, for instance. I found him on *Splodge*.

Mervin is almost monkey-like, with coarse black wires sprouting from the usual places. He is one of the hairiest men I've ever seen. In addition to the rug-like quality of his chest, armpits and limbs, this man's carpet extends to his shoulders. His back fur is evenly distributed, something I prefer to patchy hirsutism.

Mervin's neck is covered. There's no hairline at the lower boundary of his skull. You could braid his neck tufts into a French-plait, although I've never tried. The time Mervin and I have together is too precious to waste on non-erotic activity. Although it might ... never mind.

Luckily, Mervin has a full *head* of hair.

Another man I found on *Splodge* was hairy except for a pink dome on top of his head. That hadn't been the only odd thing about the guy. Before I met him, I'd thought *that* sort of anatomical variation was a myth, but I digress.

Mervin is willing to go the extra mile to provide me with new experiences, and for that reason alone, I keep moving him to the top of my list ahead of his turn.

I have to be careful, as there are *two* men called Mervin on my list. Let's refer to this one as Mervin H, to distinguish him from Mervin U (Hairy and Un-hairy respectively – their real surnames begin with the same letter, which complicates things further. I won't divulge any more, in case you know one of them.) But see, I'm digressing again.

~

My sister Zoë is having a shitty time. Her marriage is rocky. Her grown-up sons are causing grief. They're smashing cars, running up debts, experiencing minor trouble with the law, that sort of thing. Both boys live with their parents

Zoë's waste-of-space husband Darren is useless, so she likes Otto and me to spend time with her sons. She thinks we'll be a good influence. Given that I had brushes with authority when I was younger, my sister believes Den and Don relate to me.

"After all, you turned out all right, didn't you, Zeb?" she says. My mother has a different opinion about that, but we won't go there. Let her stick to pruning her bloody roses and playing bridge. She can leave me alone.

The young men enjoy spending time with Otto and me, despite the homophobic slurs they make at times. It's a classic case of *it's all right because we know you.* And I haven't digressed again. My sister's situation is relevant to my situation with Mervin.

Zoë calls on Tuesday morning. Otto is doing an online crossword, and I'm making sandwiches for my pretend work shift later that afternoon. My sister asks if we can to go to their place for dinner this evening.

"I'm busy," I tell her.

"Oh, but you have to come," she says.

"Can't," I reply. "I have something arranged."

"Well, un-arrange it," she says, "for me, Zeb." She reminds of a particularly pushy squeeze called Johan who I had to dump a few months back.

"Why," I ask. "What's the deal? Why does it have to be tonight?"

"It's complicated."

Darren and Zoë have their wedding anniversary, she explains. Somehow I've managed to forget that as well as missing my own earlier in the year. Darren says he wants to go to a rugby match with his mates, and Zoë won't have a bar of it. She's insisting on a family celebration. She anticipates stony silences if she were to dine alone with her husband. My sister explains Den or Don, I forget which, can't see why he has to be there. Zoë has told him Otto and I are coming, so he *must* be there too, or he'll ruin the party.

"Please come," she whispers. "I don't know what Darren's doing, but I think he's up to no good. I need you – " A voice interrupts her. "It won't be the same without you, Zeb," she finishes brightly.

So she's inviting Otto and me retrospectively to something that has fuck all to do with us, in an attempt to keep her loathsome husband from doing something dodgy. We have no choice but to say yes.

She says *please* the way she used to when we were kids. I want to smack her, or pull her hair like I did when we were little, only she's on the phone, so I can't. Plus since adulthood, I've reserved hair pulling for different situations. It's not something I'd do with Zoë anymore.

She changes the subject to food. "Oh, and cheese is a good idea. Perhaps that *lemon fetish* you brought at Christmas. Everyone loved that."

"Did I say I would bring cheese?" My exasperation turns my stomach in knots.

"Yes. Cheese is a great suggestion, Zeb." She speaks as if the conversation is for the benefit of a third party. "Definitely bring cheese."

Otto walks into the lounge with a hot water bottle clutched to his chest. He gesticulates in a *what's happening* way.

"It's Zoë," I say, cupping my hand over the mouthpiece. "Wants us to go over tonight, but we can't."

"Zeb?" Zoë asks. "You still there?"

"I'm checking with Otto. He's busy too." I give my husband a pleading look, but he doesn't read it. Instead, he takes the phone from me.

"Zoë, darling!" He peers at the calendar next to the fridge. "Dinner? Tonight? Of course we can."

Fuck.

"Zeb's working this afternoon, but he can join us when he's finished." He gives me a *can't you?* look.

They talk about cheese and wine. There's a certainty in Otto's words. This is happening.

Fuck fuckety.

"Yes. The *lemon fetish*," Otto says. "I'll pop into the deli. See you at seven."

Fuckety-fuck-winkles from fucktown.

~

I'm not working this afternoon. I'm meeting Mervin H.

Of course my sister would have no appreciation of the fact that I might not want to go to her stupid dinner party, because I want to get up to no good and do something dodgy myself.

I've already concocted my excuses. We've booked a room. It's not often I have to work late on a Tuesday afternoon, but if there are lot of orders and people are on annual leave, and because of how my contract works, I won't bore you with the details, but it's plausible.

Mervin H has taken the afternoon off work. He's told his wife he'll be working into the evening, there's an overdue contract, but he can't be *too* late.

Roxanne is suspicious.

She thinks Mervin has a girlfriend. The Tuesday afternoon slot arouses less suspicion, and it's good for me, since I'm not actually needed at work until Wednesday.

Sometimes I feel guilty, but I don't see myself as a home wrecker. I don't want to take Mervin away from Roxanne and their two hairy children. Rather, I see myself as the lubricant that maintains their union by oiling his wheels of lust. It's rather like the undertaker I was seeing who was married with two kids: recreational sex only. Roxanne may have no idea what's missing in their marriage, but it's not a girlfriend Mervin needs. If only she knew she didn't have to keep tabs on him.

I don't have such a problem with Otto. What with my

flexible hours, and our relative independence, it's not difficult arranging my liaisons. To be honest, my husband probably wouldn't give a shit if I'd walked in with a bunch of used sex toys in a clear plastic bag. Otto is idle and set in his ways. If he's concentrating on a crossword, or binge watching something on television, he doesn't question my comings and goings. Comings in particular, when we haven't done it for a while and he's expecting a big load, but I'll leave you to imagine how I explain that away.

Otto has stopped asking where I go. I suppose I could test the waters by bringing Mervin H home and banging him on the lounge rug in front of my husband, but he'd probably only ask us to keep it quiet, so we don't interrupt his viewing.

There are times I almost *wish* Otto would notice. Juggling my real and secret lives isn't too taxing, though it can make me anxious. But then, if we had an open relationship, would I miss the subterfuge? Sneaking around can be exhilarating.

I came home after an encounter once. Having forgotten to pack my toiletries bag, even I could smell the funk of sex coming off my body. Otto had said something about it, and I'd felt horny all over again, knowing my husband could sense the evidence.

"Shall I buy that smelly cheese you like as well as the *lemon fetish*?"

"Huh?"

I've been lost in my thoughts.

"*Epoisse de Bourgogne*, along with the *lemon fetish* for tonight?" Otto asks.

"Uh, yes." I place my sandwiches in my bag, alongside the new butt plug. It's shaped like a lemon. I found it on *marzon.co.au*, via a link from the fruit page on *Splodge.org*. "That'd be great." I walk out of the house towards the bus stop.

Mervin H is already at the hotel when I arrive. He jigs his knee up and down like a woodpecker's beak. He's wearing his work suit. He's trimmed his beard.

If he was anxious, it dissipates once we've undressed each other. He lays a tiny wafer on each of my nipples, and works his tongue round and round the left one, as if homing in on a target.

"What are those?" I gasp as one of the little squares disappears into Mervin's mouth. His teeth work, and his Adam's apple dances as he swallows. Lying beside me, he places the other one onto my lips.

"A present," he says. "You like new experiences."

Taking the thing into my mouth, I chew as he did. It tastes like nothing, has a papery texture.

"Now swallow," he commands, so I do. Then I flip over so I'm on top of him, and push my fingers through the wheat field on his belly. The room is silent apart from our breathing and the distant hum of cars. There's a tune playing in my head. The beat gets faster and faster. I lick him in places I've never tasted before. Faster. Until.

"Now swallow," he commands again.

~

We don't have much time. There are things I want to try with Mervin H. It doesn't take long until I'm on the edge again. But I need to hold back for this to work. Hold. Back.

Visualising Mum pruning roses is like the slap of a wet towel. I need something to distract me, not turn my stomach. I focus on what I'm doing later. Visiting my annoying sister. Why does she care what useless Darren does? I slow my breathing.

In my visualisation Zoë and Roxanne know each other.

Mervin examines the new toy and giggles. "Is this how?" And then, oh my god.

"Slowly!" I scream.

Zoë and Roxanne are having coffee. They both believe their husbands might be having affairs. Neither woman knows how complex this spider web of inter-connection is.

I clip the thought, return to the present.

Mervin H has pulled back and is shaking. He's laughing.

"What?" I ask.

"Isn't it funny?"

"Isn't what funny?" I feel like giggling too, but I don't know what I'm laughing at.

"Shut up and lick me again," he says, so I chow down on his nipple. It's so furry. He pushes his arms above his head, grasps the headboard. I edge up towards his armpit, enjoying the muskiness of his scent. I've done this before. We both enjoy it. I chew the hairs, sucking, licking. I'm absorbing him and being absorbed by him.

And then I stop.

Ouch.

"Don't stop," he says. "Ow! What's happening?"

"Aaaaeeee."

"What?"

"Aaaaeeeeeeee."

"What's going on?"

"Aaaaeeeeeeeeoooooow." My head follows every movement he makes. I thump him, hope he'll realise he has ... to ... stay ... still. Stay still long enough for me to untangle my tongue barbell. It's the one that has a little snake on it, and perhaps that's why it's caught up in Mervin H's hair in such a bizarre way. Every time I move, he winces and I squeal, a bizarre strangulated open-mouthed moan.

After we disconnect, I re-attach the snake piercing in the bathroom, though it's hard to insert the post into the hole, because I'm laughing so much.

Mervin takes a piss that goes on forever, and then he slips his arms around me. I turn to face him, and we laugh uncontrollably, until my face is wet. I lick his laughter tears, and at that moment, Mervin H is all I want.

"What's happening?" I ask. "What was that thing?"

"What thing?"

"The paper square?"

"Haven't you done acid before, Zeb?"

What the fuck?

"Shit. How long does this last?"

"As long as you want it to, babe," he says. "This thing can last as long as you want, as long as she never finds out." And then he's off again, giggling mercilessly.

And how long is that? There are plenty more men on *Splodge.org*. This only has to carry on as long as I want it to. But I think that might be quite a long time.

Time.

It's half past six. I'm supposed to be at Zoë's at seven! Extricating myself from Mervin, I pull my clothes on and jog to the bus stop.

There are patterns on the bus shelter walls that weren't there before, or at least I've never noticed them. Dragons are intertwining with other dragons, rusty tails twisting around each other. My mouth feels scratchy, and there are balloons inflating and deflating in my tummy, and here's the bus. A dragon sticks its tongue out at me as I walk away.

Pulling my fingers through my hair, I wonder whether I look as dishevelled as I feel. Everything feels loose. There's a swarm of insects in my stomach. Otto had said something about cheese. What was it? Did I say I would bring cheese, or did he say he would? The bus is a carousel.

I almost miss the stop. The route to Zoë and Darren's is as familiar as my own arm, and yet I feel as if I am discovering it for the first time.

Otto comes to the door when I knock.

"What kept you? We're about to eat," he says.

I stifle a giggle and follow him in. "You know how it is," I say. "They ask you to calibrate one pH meter, and suddenly there are five in front of you. I had to – " But he's stopped listening, as I knew he would. He always stops when I bombard him with a boring work story.

I pick a hair out from between my teeth before Zoë greets me. The hair is black and wiry. The urge to start laughing again is so powerful that I have to summon the image of Mum and the roses again.

It's going to be a long night.

Gone

I should have held onto him this time, but I didn't know how.

When Ronan came back to me, I'd been waiting for him for almost a decade. I always knew he'd return. But he's left me again.

I haven't been able to face work in the two weeks since he went. I rang in sick. Later, I said I'd fallen while running in the park. Eventually my lies disintegrated, and they fired me.

I didn't care.

This morning, I changed out of yesterday's clothes, cleaned my teeth and showered for the first time in days. I sprayed myself with the lily-of-the-valley scent he'd bought me when we'd found each other again. Then I took the stack of empty bottles out and went for a run in the afternoon sun. I needed the heat, wanted to feel something.

The house smells like a sewer. I must find another job. But first I have to clean up.

I bump into my ex-husband at the carwash café. As I'm out of work, I probably should clean the car myself. But since I bought the Honda, I've had her valeted regularly, as if by looking after the car, I'm also caring for myself.

Abe is friendly enough, even buys me coffee. I ask about our son. Kyle's partner is active on social media, so I know we've had a second grandchild. Abe tells me the baby is babbling and reaching out for toys. He updates me as if I'm an outsider, like an old neighbour, or perhaps someone who once taught Kyle at school, not his fucking mother.

We talk about Abe's work, his in-laws in France. There's an easy confidence between us, as if once being married has stripped away our shyness. Things can go the other way with an ex, but we parted without hating each other. It happened a long time ago, before Ronan. Perhaps we'd married too young.

"Are you still living in the same place, Madeleine?" He drains his coffee.

"I don't ever want to leave." I remember the two of us painting every room when we moved in years ago. Abe likely has no idea how close I've come to losing that house. He knows I was forced to leave teaching after my *indiscretion* was discovered. I've flitted from one low wage job to another, often working two together. I'm determined to keep my home, despite the crippling mortgage and having an arsehole of a neighbour. It's where I raised our son. And it's where Ronan and I have been at our happiest. We might have stayed there until one of us died if he hadn't left me again.

~

Abe is a good man. He doesn't judge me as everyone else does. It's as if the turmoil of being rejected by our son, kissing my career goodbye, and being pointed at in the street is someone else's fault. I suspect Abe was pleased when I started a relationship with someone, even though that someone was a child. It let him off the hook.

When most people were demonising me, Abe and his wife Sondrine were supportive. As a stepmother, Sondrine offered to talk to Kyle, to encourage him to speak to me. Kyle hasn't followed her advice.

The distance between my son and me is an ocean. He doesn't need me. He has his father. He shares good times and bad times with Abe and Sondrine. Kyle has never forgiven me for falling in love with his best friend.

Abe talks about Sondrine's sister's new partner, and asks whether I have anyone special in my life.

"Not just now," I reply. I can't face telling him there was someone until very recently. I make an unnecessary trip to the bathroom, so Abe won't see my tears.

When we reunited, Ronan asked to take things slowly. He wanted to keep our relationship *private* until the right time.

The time never came. When I pushed for a decision, he was cruel.

"I don't know what I ever saw in you, Madeleine," he said.

"But you love me," I'd pleaded. "You know you do."

"I never should have come back."

"We were so happy. Remember?"

"I was never sure about you." He'd turned his back on me. "I wish I hadn't wasted my youth on you."

Youth. That had stung.

I'd understand the pull of a wife and children. But Ronan isn't going back to wretched Gretchen and their children. He's left me for an office girl he'd been seeing behind Gretchen's back. She's just turned eighteen; not much older than Ronan was himself when I first took him to my bed.

After I return from the bathroom, Abe asks if I want another coffee. Our cars are ready, he says, but he doesn't have much else to do. He can stay for a bit. Do I have the time, he asks. We haven't seen each other for a while, he says, adding that it's good to chat.

"I have all the time in the world." I order the drinks.

"Does Burt Hartley still live next door?" Abe asks when I come back.

"Unfortunately."

"I thought he'd be dead by now."

"Trust me," I say. "He would be if I had anything to do with it."

Abe laughs and we talk about how Burt might die, complicit in our murderous thoughts. I imagine a giant boulder rolling down the hill, crashing into Burt's house, missing mine by centimeters. Abe suggests wild mushroom poisoning. Burt is a forager. We laugh, and I love how easy it is between us. I wish Kyle could share this. I wonder what it would be like if we'd stayed together. But the idea is unappealing.

There's only one person I want, and that person has left me. Again.

Perhaps Ronan will come back. He's returned so many times before.

But this time, there's something different in the way he's severed our ties.

This time, I think he may have gone for good.

A Girl Called Miranda

Taz was drunk the day I met him.

I liked him instantly.

This lanky guy pulled a stool across the beer-splashed floor and knocked the tiny table where Rishan and I were sitting.

"This is Asher." Rishan cocked his head towards me. "You know. The one I told you about." Looking at me, he said, "This is Taz."

"We meet at last." The guy reached for my hand and gave it a squeeze. I took in the blue-black hair, the Led Zeppelin T-shirt, the way his eyes didn't quite meet yours when he spoke.

"You work with Rish. That right?"

"Part time." I shifted my chair so he could move closer to the table. "I'm studying."

"I'll get a round in," Rishan said. "And some chips."

"And get me a pickled egg, would you?" Taz smiled.

"Okay." Rishan wound his way through the crowd. The bar was thick with people.

Taz turned back and faced slightly to the left of me, so I wasn't sure if he was talking to me or someone else. "Been back in Yorkshire over a week, and I haven't had a fucking pickled egg yet."

"Don't do it," I said. "They're the devil's food."

143

We were in that old pub near the waterworks. I forget the name. People had chucked empty crisp packets into the unlit inglenook fireplace. Dusk was falling. Multi-coloured lights twinkled like distant traffic.

"I've heard a lot about you." Rishan's friend pulled my sleeve away from a spreading pool of beer on the table. "You keep that one out of trouble?" He cocked his head in Rishan's direction.

"Other way round. And he never stops talking about you," I said, taking a cigarette from his pack.

"All good, I hope." We made eye contact then. I guess you could describe the way he looked at me as wistful. It made me think he'd seen things I hadn't; that he knew things I didn't.

I hardly ever touched a cigarette back then. Couldn't afford them. Taz didn't seem to mind that I'd helped myself from his pack, even though he only had two left.

Rishan came back with beer.

Taz asked what I was doing at uni. I glossed over the details of my course, didn't want to have that conversation about how it would lead to nothing. Nowhere. I steered the conversation towards music. Told him I'd just bought the new *U2* album. He asked if I liked South American music. I said I didn't know.

The guy talked about panpipes, about ballet, about Pinochet and the Chicago Boys, a bunch of Chilean economists in the seventies. He told me about the forced *disappearances* of political opponents. People destined never to be seen again. I would have been out of my depth if anyone else had been talking about those things. I knew nothing about politics. But the way Taz poured the words out made them interesting. Important. I promised I'd search the library and learn more, though even as I said it, I knew I'd never find time.

The food arrived – chips as fat as thumbs. Rishan drowned his plate in ketchup like he always did. Taz said he'd be leaving England again before long, something about a trip to Germany, if he could find the cash. He drained his pint and headed for the toilet, walking in spidery zigzags. On the way back, he put *Tainted Love* on the jukebox, and then he told us a story about sheep. He'd been working at a sheep station in southwest Australia for two years. That's why I hadn't met him yet, even though he was Rishan's best mate.

We shared his last cigarette, cupped our hands around it like we were smoking weed. The beer slid down our throats too easily. Taz gave me a wet kiss when I told the Quasimodo joke, one of my standards. There were more hugs when I laughed at his. Even so, he was tentative, as if scared he might catch something from me. But I only sensed that from close in. From the outside, no one would have seen his hesitance as he bear-hugged me, like I was a long-lost sister.

The music stopped, and Taz said something to Rishan about a girl called Miranda.

Rishan's face coloured. You could tell, even in the low lights of the bar.

"Best night of my life," Taz said, though he sounded sad, not happy. His speech was slurring, and his eyes red.

A bell signalled time. We needed to drink up and leave.

"Okay mate. Time we got going." Rishan hugged his friend. Most of the punters ignored the bell, carried on shouting, sipping their drinks slowly. Rishan squeezed my knee under the table and said he'd walk me home. I couldn't read his expression. Didn't know whether he'd leave me at my door when we got there, or if he'd come in. He didn't usually decide until he reached my flat.

The barman roared another warning. There was a clang of breaking glass.

We liked that bar near the waterworks. Sometimes Rishan and I would go there on his bike; the engine's roar echoing through the underpass like a chainsaw. We'd play pool. He'd drink more than he ought to. Then we'd head to my place and fuck. Afterwards he'd ride back to the city, to Anita.

The next time Taz came out with us, he was already drunk, as he had been the last time. When Rishan went to the bar, Taz kissed my face, just brushing my lips. I tasted his salt and wondered if there was more to his affection than alcohol. I would have thought he was making a pass, except Rishan had recently discovered Taz was gay.

He'd told Rishan about his few tentative relationships with men. There was a boyfriend in Australia. I wasn't certain if Taz *only* went for guys. He'd had girlfriends in the past. As far as *he* knew, I was single. Good for a laugh. Available.

Taz had mentioned the girl called Miranda again that night. Rishan brushed the subject aside again. Perhaps he hadn't liked this woman. Perhaps he'd been jealous because she'd taken his best mate away for a while.

I didn't know if Rishan had told Taz about *our* relationship. A knowing look had passed between them on the night we were introduced. Did Taz know? And if he did, why was he flirting with me? The pantomime nature of Taz's next kiss told me there was no serious intent behind his exaggerated gestures. His actions sat somewhere between pretence and lies.

That suited me.

Back then, the only person I wanted was Rishan.

Taz and I bumped into each other one night when I was walking home from the library. He'd been back from Australia a few months by then. We stopped in the Fav for a drink. I wanted to ask him about Rishan. I needed to learn more about my lover – the man who was someone else's boyfriend. I wanted to know if there was any chance he'd leave Anita. But Taz wanted to talk about himself. People so often do.

When Taz had worked on the sheep station in Australia, he'd made a balls-up of it. I'd heard some of the stories from Rishan, but I liked hearing them directly from Taz, laced with the mild Australian accent he'd acquired.

He'd nearly maimed an ewe at his first attempt at shearing. He'd fed a sheepdog chocolate and almost killed it. He'd left a gate open, and a flock of sheep had disappeared. He'd driven one of the station vehicles into a gully.

He asked what I wanted to do after college, but I turned the conversation, pushed him to talk about when he and Rishan were kids.

Taz was Rishan's best friend. They would drop stones on the railway from the bridge near Tophouse Avenue. Taz would persuade Rishan to steal cigarettes for him from the corner shop. They'd often liked the same girl, but Taz would back off.

Rishan usually got what he wanted. It seems he hadn't changed.

Except there was one time, Taz said, they'd had to share. The details were sketchy. Something about a threesome with a girl from school called Miranda, one of them at either end of her. Head to toe to head. The thought made me strangely jealous, even though jealousy wasn't part of my relationship with Rishan. I had to live with his being Anita's boyfriend, not mine, from day one.

"Ah, Miranda, Miranda," Taz said, pushing a hand through his spiky black hair. "Miranda, My-randa." He giggled to himself, as if I wasn't there.

I pressed for more, but it was Taz's turn to switch the conversation.

"How long have you known Rish?" There was something challenging about the way he asked it.

"Not as long as you," I replied. "But I know him well. Really well." I'd provided an opening, an opportunity for Taz to say, *yes, he told me about you two.*

But instead, he said something cryptic. "Sometimes people aren't who you think they are. Sometimes they want something different from what you think they do."

I had to leave soon after that. Had a test I needed to study for.

How long *had* I known Rishan?

We met soon after I started uni, when I began working at the *Splendour Palace* bar. I didn't fancy Rishan, even though he was slim, hair dyed blonde, lean-limbed with baby-soft skin, just the way I like my men. I didn't think of him in *that* way, but I liked how he made us laugh. He joked with the customers, put them at ease, and flattered the women.

Rishan talked about Taz all the time. He had us in hysterics, telling stories about how his mate had shaved the hair off his gonads after losing a bet, how he'd nicked the skin in the process.

And he told us the sheep stories.

Taz used to write to Rishan regularly. It wasn't a thing most of my guy-friends did, but I guess they were close. Rishan would bring the letters to work and share parts – anything for a laugh.

We heard how Taz had mended a dog-fence and messed up. They reckoned dingoes had entered that night and taken several lambs. They found one carcass, but six disappeared, never to be seen again. It wasn't so long since some baby had gone missing in Ayers Rock. Everyone had a point of view about that story, even though none of us had been there.

Our colleagues would ask if he'd had another letter yet. They looked forward to the stories, especially the ones about sheep.

There was one letter Rishan only shared with me. It came about a year before Taz returned. He'd met a guy called Baradine. He said they were 'dating'. Oddly quaint.

I didn't know why I was the only one Rishan showed the letter to. I guess it was because we were getting close, getting jokes others didn't, finishing each other's sentences, that sort of thing. An electrical charge was mounting between us. He trusted me. He wasn't embarrassed his friend had come out of the closet, but there was something there. Some deep unseated hurt that showed in his eyes.

I wondered if he felt Taz was letting the side down. I'd never have picked Rishan as homophobic, but he made me wonder that day. I told him not to dwell on it. I wanted to kiss his hurt away, but didn't know if I could.

A few days after the letter, we'd just fitted a new keg in the basement, and Rishan had leant against the wall. He'd pushed his legs across the passage, blocking my exit up to the bar. There was something peculiar about the way he'd been looking at me.

"What?" I'd asked.

"I like you," he said. He looked as if he was about to pass out. People never said anything like that when sober.

"Yeah?" The blood had rushed to my cheeks and made them warm. "I like you too. The customers will be here soon."

"No, Asher. I mean I *really* like you."

I'd let out a nervous giggle. Rishan had Anita. But he put his hand on my shoulder and asked if I liked him. It was child-like, almost sweet.

"Of course I do, dick." I'd mock-punched him. "Let's get back upstairs."

He hadn't let me pass.

And I hadn't wanted him to.

"Really?"

"Really."

We lunged at each other with a hunger that wouldn't stop for years.

But he didn't leave Anita. He wouldn't.

Rishan had been with Anita since they were teenagers. On and off. Off and on.

She fell pregnant a few months after our relationship began, a sordid reminder that what Rishan was doing with me, he'd been doing with her too.

They decided to marry. I went to the wedding, drank so much cider, I was sick on my new frock. Anita remained sober and serene throughout. I don't remember how I made my way home. I woke in my own bed the next day with a mother of a hangover.

After the wedding, Rishan's wife occasionally came to the bar to meet her husband. She'd push her belly ahead of her like a prized pumpkin, even though she was barely showing. She'd chat to the bar staff, and flirt with the men by the jukebox.

"You okay?" Rishan would ask after she left.

"What do you think?"

I guess he knew I was upset, though he likely never sensed how much I burned.

Rishan finally left Anita when their kid Sam was eighteen months old. I should have felt wretched. Guilty. But I didn't. I felt vindicated. I'd got what I wanted.

Taz was back from Germany, but we didn't see much of him after we became an official couple. Apparently he'd *sided with* Anita, and was being frosty.

"He'll get over it," I said, but I saw the hurt in Rishan's eyes. I'd only seen that look on a handful of occasions.

Taz left the area soon afterwards.

Our son Ali was born a year after Rishan moved out of the marital home.

I had everything I wanted, but life has a strange way of getting its own back. I guess we struggled with the baby in the tiny flat with its leaky walls and problems with vermin. I suppose I had even more of a problem with Rishan's wandering eye.

Ali was two when Rishan said he'd fallen in love with Kirsten, the new Saturday girl. She was still at school.

~

Anita and I bumped into each other at the playground not long afterwards. Sam and Ali were taking turns pushing each other on a roundabout. They'd never met before.

Anita came up to me. "Look at them," she said. "You'd think they knew they were brothers." We got chatting. The animosity between us had evaporated after so long. We agreed to meet up again, so the boys could form a bond.

After a few months, when I felt brave enough, I asked Anita about Miranda. She reckoned there hadn't been anyone called Miranda at school. She must have forgotten. Maybe she knew about the threesome, but was embarrassed her ex-husband had done something so unwholesome. Perhaps it had happened when she and Rishan were together. If she had a point of view about *that* story, she wasn't sharing it.

Taz and I reconnected recently.

I was in Leicester for a meeting. Saw him walking near the train station. I clocked his pipe-cleaner legs and newborn foal walk, before I recognised his features.

"Taz?" We hesitated before hugging. He was looking at a spot behind my head.

"Asher!" He gave me a warm-wet kiss, and then coughed.

We had a drink at a bar near the station, while I waited for my train. I'd often wondered how Taz had got on after he'd left town. But we'd heard nothing from him for years. No one had.

"How's Rishan?" He looked hopeful, as if I was the only link to his old friend.

"I only see him as much as I need to," I said. "Things to do with our son. Haven't you been in contact recently?"

"A son! So you guys finally got together." He smiled. "But you're not with each other anymore?"

"Nah. Enough about me," I steered the conversation around. "What about you? Any love in your life?"

"I'm with someone called David."

We talked about David. I crunched an ice cube from my drink.

"Is he the love of your life, Taz?"

"No. There's only ever been the one." He coughed again.

"So who was the special one? Was it Baradine?"

"No. Someone else."

"Who? Tell me." My train was due in ten minutes. "I have to go soon."

"Can't you guess?"

"I can't."

I made out I had no idea, but I knew. I couldn't prove it, but I knew.

We agreed to stay in touch.

Taz rang me three weeks ago, for the first time in months. He cut straight to the point.

"I've had bad news." He sounded as if a cork had been pulled from his body and the air had escaped.

"I'm sorry."

"It's lung cancer. Guess that's why I was coughing a lot."

We talked about options and the future – the lack of one.

"How's David taking it?"

"I'm not with David anymore."

"I'm sorry. I wish you had someone special in your life right now."

"Oh but I do, Asher. I do."

"A new man?"

"No. A very old one."

"Geriatric love. My favourite."

"He's not." Taz gasped for breath.

"Not what?"

"Geriatric."

"Is he looking after you?"

"He's not here." He wasn't making sense.

"Where is he?"

"He's in my heart."

At Taz's funeral, there's a photo display. I'm not sure who's put it together. People crowd around, pointing and laughing. There's one from his sheep station days. Taz is standing at a dog-fence holding a pair of clippers and grinning.

There are pictures from school. Rishan's in some, Anita's in others.

There's an official class photo, taken in their final school year. I look through the names for a girl called Miranda, but there's no sign of her.

It's like she never existed.

Analysis

My sister has discovered anal sex.

"Why didn't you tell me about this before, Zeb?" she asks. We're sipping chardonnay on her balcony. Zoë lives in the heart of the city. She's been divorced three months, and is in want of fuck buddies. It's too early to delve into anything serious, she says. She wants to have fun. "I'd have tried it before, if you'd told me how good it was."

"You never asked." I help myself to an olive. There's a slight breeze coming through, but it's still warm.

"What's the point in having a gay brother if you don't let me in on the saucy secrets?"

I don't remind Zoë it's because she used to be such a prude. She'd been married to boring Darren for so long, I can't imagine her going on the pull. Yet she has been. And she's been stemming the rose with a Greek guy called Giannis (pronounced Yannus). She met him via one of those 'no strings' apps.

We get analytical about positions and technicalities. Funny how she never used to talk like this before. Zoë's actually a lot more fun since she ditched Darren. Useless bloody Darren. So I have to ask her.

"You were married to Darren for so long. Didn't you ever – you know – try it with him?"

"Oh, we did," she says.

"But you just said – "

"We *tried*."

"And?"

"He was too big."

I am filled with a new respect for my ex-brother-in-law.

I wonder if three months is too soon for me to ask my sister to give me her ex's number.

Just Deserts

I've worked hard. I deserve everything I have. I've built this company from nothing without the benefit of a tertiary qualification. Though I'd had good grades at school, my education ended early, but I learned all I needed to know in the bed of an excommunicated schoolteacher.

My beautiful home, my lovely wife, I have it all. Svetlana and I play tennis three times a week. We travel overseas when we can. I exercise regularly, but not too hard. I eat well. I drink in moderation. I've worked on my health since I had the scare, and I'm in good shape. The company is doing well. Harry and Ness are handling the business competently, so I've been able to step back. I'm proud of all my children. Hana says Marco wants to be an accountant, and is studying hard for his exams. He'll be an asset to the company too.

Sometimes I miss the busyness of the business, but it's time to reap the benefits of my work. I've earned my early retirement.

~

I could have stopped working years ago.

I wonder how different my life would have been if my first husband hadn't left me. Would I still be struggling to pay the bills, if I didn't have the blight of divorce staining my past?

What if I hadn't destroyed my relationship with my son when I seduced his best friend? What if I hadn't committed career suicide?

Or what if my love with Ronan had lasted?

Maybe we'd binge watch television all day, or go to bed in the afternoon and stay there until sundown. Perhaps we'd go to the theatre once a month, or have front row seats for the Symphony Orchestra when they played the Town Hall.

I imagine these things, when I'm on an evening shift. Come morning, I'll be at my day job. I have a good smile I'm told, well suited to front of house.

I have no regrets.

My life could have been different, if I hadn't paid such a price for love.

But I wouldn't have wanted it any other way.

~

My mother often visits us. Sometimes she's here for the weekend, but she'll stay a whole week if her arthritis is bad. She can be snippy with Svetlana.

"Why Jacqui comes so much?" my wife asks.

I tell her it won't be forever.

There was a time I argued with my mother every day, and couldn't bear her company. But she's always been there for me. She raised me alone after my waste-of-space father left. Apparently he came and went during the first six months of my life. But I have no memory of him. As far as I'm concerned, he fucked off before I was born. It's always been Mum and me, except for the five years she didn't speak to me.

~

People ask why I never found another man. Sometimes I imagine sitting on the deck watching the sunset with a bland companion. Perhaps he's something like my first husband. I have to banish that thought. Abe was decent enough, but in some ways, I wish I'd never met him. If I'd never met him, I'd never have had Kyle, and if my son hadn't been born, then I'd never have met his best friend, and if that hadn't happened, who knows what my life would have been like? Better or worse? Worse or better?

The jury's still out on that one.

~

Sometimes I listen to two pieces of music simultaneously. I like variety.

Sometimes I think about the women I have loved.

I think about Madeleine. She wanted us to be together forever. But could I have stayed with one woman my whole life? Even her? She was a hard woman to leave. She wanted us to marry. For better, for worse. For worse, for better.

~

I haven't been to Ronan's house for a long time. I used to drive there and creep up that long driveway at dusk, right up to the window, just to look at him.

~

I haven't seen Madeleine for a long time. Sometimes I wonder what would happen if she died. She's much older than me, so it's likely she won't be around forever. Would I know? Would anyone tell me?

~

I used to think I couldn't live without Ronan. He came and went. He'd want me and then he'd discard me. If he died, would I know? I think he'd find a way to let me know he was leaving this life. I believe he'd say a final goodbye. He always promised he'd visit me in another life. But what the fuck did he know? He was just a kid.

~

I've led a good life. I deserve everything I have.

~

I've led a difficult life. It doesn't get easier. Will I smile sweetly to customers all day, and then keep that sugary demeanour as I wipe shit from the arse of someone who's only a few years older than me?

It's been hard, but I have no complaints.

I've been lucky. Most people haven't had what I had.

I've known deep love, and I deserved it.

162

~

I have three children. Maybe more. That's the hard thing about being a man. You leave parts of yourself in places you perhaps shouldn't.

~

I only had the one son. He hasn't spoken to me for half his life. I would have liked another child. Ronan and I talked about a baby. His words were always tinged with fear.

~

I'm enjoying retirement. I can't think of anything that would make my life any better. Well I can, but that's not going to happen.

I could look for her, but I'm scared what might happen if I find her.

~

I don't know if I'll ever stop working. I don't know if I'll ever stop wanting him.

~

Sometimes I have this pain in my chest, and I don't know what it is.

Well, I do know, but I won't cry about what's lost, when I have so much.

The Size of the Lie

Aunt Zoryana stands in front of my grandmother's house.

Mother is beside me and looks at her sister-in-law. She says Zoryana is a *broken woman*.

My aunt has to stick pieces of herself together, but I fear she'll find the parts no longer fit.

There is a bruise under her eye.

Father takes her suitcase, but says nothing.

We drive my aunt to the airport. She will return to her family, to an uncertain future of bare shelves and the rattle of guns at nighttime.

How things have changed in a short time. I had painted Zoryana's lips crimson on her wedding day. The elderly ladies who had dressed her said I did a good job. I absorbed the praise like bread soaks gravy.

After the wedding feast, my father lifted me onto a table.

"My daughter found the bride," he boasted, lifting my chin. "She is computer genius."

"It is true," Mother had said. "No one knows Internetting like Nadia."

Uncle Vitaly was forty years old and lived with his mother. A simple man in a complex world, he would jump at loud noises. He was frightened of mice and couldn't keep his trousers clean.

When he came to visit, he would pull my ponytail and make fun of my dolls. He spoke in the old language and called me stupid when I didn't understand him.

Before his marriage, Grandmother cooked Vitaly's meals, washed his clothes and looked after his money if he ever had any.

My uncle struggled to hold down a job. He would break machinery, argue with the boss and steal other men's boots.

My parents despaired.

When will you settle?

You should have a family.

You must look after Mother now, not she you.

There'd been no hope of a wife. No one in our community wanted an unemployable man as a husband or son-in-law, especially one who looked like a scarecrow and had dirty hands.

Grandmother said she couldn't keep him anymore. It might be different if he had a wife to help she'd said, otherwise Vitaly had to come and live with us.

I'd found the website.

"We can find Uncle Vitaly a wife." I'd beamed, clicking from page to page, so my parents couldn't see what I didn't want them to.

My mother supplied a photo. Uncle Vitaly still had hair when it was taken.

I filled in the form.

Are you fit and healthy?

Yes.

(His leg had always been like that.)

Do you have a criminal record?

No.

(The police only cautioned him for urinating from the bus shelter roof.)

Have you been married before?

No.

(I could tell the honest truth. Sometimes.)

Grandmother brought my uncle to inspect the girls on my computer. Father asked many questions.

I was careful with my omissions. The site said the girl of your dreams:

... *will keep your house tidy.*

... *always look attractive for you.*

I missed out the word *sexy* when I read that part out.

... *remembers her husband is head of the family.*

Vitaly smiled as my mother translated.

Father tutted at the cost.

Grandmother said she would be happy if her boy was happy.

Within a month I was eating wedding-cake, smiling at my new Auntie, while relatives whispered about the size of her feet and how much younger she looked in her photo.

~

It lasted three months.

We're sending Zoryana back.

Grandmother uses the word *whore* a lot. I've never heard her say it before.

Vitaly says Zoryana should have obeyed him. He is head of the family.

Father has to pay for the airfare and a lot more besides.

He takes my computer and stamps on it.

"I need that for school," I plead, but the computer is in three pieces. "They were only little lies," I cry.

"It's not the size of the lie, Nadia," Mother says, "but how far it is from the truth."

I try to piece the computer parts together, only to discover they no longer fit.

So Much Older

The other patients on the ward are so much older. Svetlana walks towards me wearing something that shows her waist to best advantage. The bastard in the bed opposite eyes her up and down. His whiskery chin and hooded eyelids remind me of Burt Hartley, a dour old man who made my life a misery for years. Svetlana would have hated him if she'd ever met him. I haven't seen the fucker in ages.

My wife is carrying grapes wrapped in cellophane.

Fucking grapes for a sick person.

Doesn't Svetlana know I hate clichés? I dislike predictability almost as much as I hate the fact I have to share this space because my condition is deemed too serious for me to be in the hospital of my choice. I can't eat grapes anyway. My 'intake' is being controlled. Little and often. Tasteless and fetid.

"Jacqui waiting outside." Svetlana kisses my cheek. I'm glad the rules limit me to one visitor at a time. I'm too weak to act as referee between my mother and wife. "I say I see you first." She places the fruit in their crinkly wrapper on the bedside cabinet. "How you are feeling?"

"I've been better."

Fucking understatement. Svetlana was with me when

the specialist outlined my options and the associated risks. She was all *Mrs. Hancock this* and *Mrs. Hancock that,* until my wife asked the doc to call her Svetlana. It's not uncommon for wives to keep their own names when they marry. People shouldn't assume.

I wish Mum had come first. I'm scared. I don't want my wife to know. Though I try to smile, Svetlana's expression suggests it is a grimace.

"Good sleep?"

I nod. The truth is an acid panic disturbed me long after 'Burt' and the others started snoring.

"Did you talk to Ness and Harry?" Fuck it's hard to push the words out.

"You can't worry for business, Ronan," she says, smoothing her hand over the beige hospital counterpane.

I flick a piece of fluff away, but it won't budge. I realise there's nothing there.

"Your kids look after," she says.

Everything is the same colour: beige curtains, beige walls, beige vomit in the bowl Burt's neighbour retches into. The man rings his buzzer again. The place stinks. The smell gives me a headache. A nurse arrives, covers the bowl and whisks it away.

Svetlana talks about tennis and throws platitudes at me, as if her good intentions alone will have me playing mixed doubles soon. *And maybe you can ... or if you ...*

I don't know how long I was asleep for. When I open my eyes, my mother is there. Svetlana has disappeared.

"Mum."

My voice is a hoarse whisper. I don't have the energy to say much.

She squeezes my hand.

"Don't speak." She smiles and I want to cry with relief. My mother used to be a benevolent dictator in our family of two. She was kind and omnipotent. She could make anything better. She *would* make everything better, except when she shunned me, because she was ashamed. Mum looks blurred around the edges. Maybe it's the medication I'm on.

"Can you hear music?" I ask.

"There's no music, Ronan. Just rest."

When I wake again, the light has changed. Something's beeping. The curtains are drawn around Burt's bed. Mum's gone. Someone runs in with a trolley. Raised voices. Scraping noises. Multiple choices. Really there aren't any choices for a man in my position. I block the sounds, and it's worse. I hear the music in my own head.

Harpsichord.

Madeleine and my mother liked Baroque music. I hated that shit.

I creep downstairs, leaving my friend Kyle in the top bunk. There's music playing on Mum's CD player. She's waving her hand, as if she's conducting an orchestra.

Madeleine's there.

"You should be asleep shouldn't you, honey?" She

smiles that smile, and I'm what, twelve years old. I'm already in love with her. Have been since summer. The guilt kills me, and I can't talk to anyone about it. She's my friend's mother. I want to be near her. Can't sleep, because Burt is snoring too much, but Burt is already dead.

"It's all right," the nurse says. He's the one who whisked the vomit pot away. How long ago was that? "Just breathe."

The sharp pain is back. I try to tell him. But pain is my friend. I want it, because while I feel pain, I'm alive.

The nurse checks readings and ticks things.

"Do you need anything for the pain?"

"No."

"How bad is it?"

"Eleven out of ten." Every breath is more painful than the last.

"You're a bit off colour," he says. "I'll get Dr Khan to have a look."

"Don't go."

"I won't be long."

"Where's Madeleine?"

"Huh? Back in a minute."

"Tell her. Make sure you tell her. Tell ..." but I've run out of breath.

A machine beeps as she pulls the curtain aside.

"Madeleine."

"Don't speak." She smiles and I want to cry with

relief.

"You came." I'm speaking, but I don't have a voice. "I always thought – because you're so much older – you'd go first."

She puts a finger to her lips. I catch her scent when she leans over to kiss me. The beige, the beeping, the biliousness and Baroque music disappear. She reminds me of those little white flowers I can never remember the name of. They come in spring. I once bought her a perfume that carried their fragrance. What are they called? Lily-of-the-something. I taste electricity on her tongue.

Stand clear.

She's telling them to leave us. I push them away using the power of my mind.

Madeleine is with me.

I'm so happy I could die.

Incest by Proxy

When he tells me his real name is Giannis, pronounced *Yannus,* it triggers a memory. I'd wanted someone new. Not a problem with *Splodge.org.* You can find any man you want there. I have a list of guys I see on a regular basis, but occasionally I like to dip my toe (and other bits) into something different, so that's why I'd visited new parts of the site.

I don't recognise the man's face. I'm sure I'd have remembered him if we'd fucked before. I'd have remembered those sculpted pecs, the velvet eyes, the way his cock curves to the right when he's hard. And yet there is something familiar about his name.

I try my lemon butt plug on Giannis, and he approves. The windows of the hotel room have steamed up. It's cold outside. He's brought a bag of toys too. I feed his hardness into the vampire fleshlight. He squeals when it bites. Then he fits the neoprene quick restraints on me, but there's nothing quick about what he does next. My turn to scream. The puppy hoods make us laugh.

Soon it will be time to go. I should probably get home before nightfall. There is never enough time.

"You didn't tell me your real name," he says as I'm dressing.

For a second I consider lying, as if there is a reason he

mustn't know who I really am. "Zeb," I say. I don't tell him my surname, and he doesn't ask. "Zeb," I repeat. "Short for Zebedee. It means *gift from God.*"

"Are your parents religious, Zeb?" He's tying his shoelaces, sitting on the bed, leaning forward so I can see the top of his head. I want to kiss it, but if we start again, we'll be late. We only have the room for another fifteen minutes.

"Not really," I tell him. "They liked names starting with the letter 'Z'. My sister is called Zoë. Dad's dead now, and Mum doesn't care about anything except her roses. Never been regular church goers or anything."

"Zoë." He scratches his beard. "I dated a woman called Zoë. Not so long ago."

I know Giannis swings both ways. At least that is what his *Splodge.org* profile states. But you never know what truths people choose to reveal on the site, and what they make up in order to attract what they think they want.

"Do you want to do this again?"

"I'll let you know," he says.

I shouldn't have asked. Should have been patient and contacted him through *Splodge*. I've left myself open. He's rejected me to my face. *I'll let you know* has never meant anything but *it's been nice knowing you.*

He's at the door and looks back at me. There is something unnerving about the way he hesitates.

"It's been fun," he says. "I enjoyed the lemon."

"Me too," I say, not certain which of the toys we used I liked most, or whether I only relished being in the presence of someone so hot.

"Say *Hi* to Zoë," he says, and then he's gone.

Although it's cold, I decide to walk home. It's probably warmer than waiting for the bus. Otto is planning to cook a beef hotpot tonight.

Why did Giannis specifically ask me to say *Hi* to Zoë?

Otto serves his hotpot with pickled gherkin. You wouldn't think they'd go well together, but hotpot and pickle are a hit in our house.

Mentioning Zoë as we parted was odd. Giannis doesn't know her.

I've always liked Otto's pickled gherkin.

Or *does* Giannis know my sister?

Recently I've been wondering whether I want to stay with my husband. Otto and I have been together almost thirty years. Or is it more? Shit. I should know.

That time when Zoë and I were drinking wine on her balcony. Didn't she say she'd been seeing a Greek guy? What was his name?

I'm not sure if the relationship is coming to a natural end, or whether I just want more. More than Otto can give.

Giannis. Giannis pronounced *Yannus*. Wasn't that it?

I want more than Otto can give, but does that mean I don't want him?

Did Giannis fuck both of us? Me and my sister?

I want both.

Why does that feel as if sharing Giannis was wrong?

After all, haven't I lusted after Zoë's other partners in the past?

Why does it feel as if I need to make a decision? After all, haven't I been leading this double life for some time now?

I won't say *Hi* to Zoë from Giannis. And I'm not going to contact him again.

Otto opens the door, and the aroma of the hotpot comforts me. Is that what it is? Do I stay with him because I'm *comfortable?*

"Zoë dropped by," he says, "visiting someone local. Wondered if we were in."

"How was she?" I ask.

"She's okay," Otto says. "Says she's had a bad back, but she's comfortable now."

"That's good to know," I say. "I'm glad."

Otto pulls a seat out for me. "Sit. Dinner's ready."

"Thanks. Yes, *comfortable* is good." I dip a spoon into the hotpot.

It tastes divine.

Unspoken Words

They're playing Chopin's *Marche Funèbre.*

Ronan would have hated it. He didn't like clichés.

Maybe his children chose the music. Harry and Ness sit on the front pew with their mother. It's years since Gretchen and Ronan divorced, but she looks miserable. Perhaps someone thought music suited to a nineteen-fifties cartoon would lighten the mood: someone with a warped sense of humour and a liking for irony.

Harry and Ness are dressed in anti-funereal colours. I can't see their faces. Their silhouettes are as familiar as my own son's. I watched them from afar when they were small.

I used to watch their mother, too. Gretchen doesn't look much older than she did when she married Ronan. The funeral is in the same church, the congregation bathed in the same stained glass light, and the same uninvited guest sits at the back. Only this time I've collected an order of service at the entrance. Ronan looks youthful in the photos. Why wouldn't he? They say only the good die young. Ronan hated clichés. Perhaps it's appropriate he doesn't fit that one.

He wasn't a good man.

I went to his first wedding wishing he'd chosen me instead.

Today, I attend his funeral with a sense of acceptance.

Ronan's youngest child sits behind Harry and Ness. The pamphlet tells me he's called Marco, though I don't need the piece of paper to know his name. I've watched Marco too. His mother Hana is only a decade or so older than Gretchen's son and daughter. Ronan had employed his second wife as an intern. I discovered he'd been screwing Hana when we were together the second time. He always had an eye for young flesh, but that's hardly something I can criticise him for.

I didn't like Ronan's first wife. I despised Hana even more. When Ronan married Gretchen it almost broke me. But he eventually left her and came back to me. When he left me for Hana, I wanted to die. I felt she deserved his affection less than Gretchen did, though there was no rational reason for the difference.

Wife number three, the widow, is called Svetlana. She's tall, with an athletic build. Svetlana is dressed as if she's auditioning for a part in an action movie. By the time Ronan married her, I'd stopped driving to his property to look at him. Well, there may have been the occasional lapse, but I'd accepted I had to let him go. Sometimes, though, I sensed he hadn't released me. He may still have been watching me, though I'll never know for sure. We were never good at letting go.

It's not easy to identify people when you see them from behind. A crooked woman sits close to Svetlana. She might be Jacqui. Ronan's mother's stooped back makes her look older than she is. It's hard to tell from here, especially under her oversized hat. Jacqui always had a sense of the theatrical. There's an unoccupied space between her and Svetlana, as if they're waiting for Ronan to climb out of his coffin and join them.

Jacqui used to be my best friend. When she discovered I'd been having a relationship with Ronan since he was fifteen years old, she didn't speak to him for five years. She hasn't spoken to *me* since. Jacqui wasn't the only casualty of our relationship, but I have grown accustomed to not having my son anymore.

Ronan rarely mentioned his mother when he lived with me. For five years, Jacqui's name only came up in arguments. He'd had a love/hate relationship with her. Sometimes it seemed I missed Jacqui more than Ronan did.

The celebrant invites Harry to the lectern. He doesn't say much, focussing on Ronan's achievements, the construction company he built, the legacy he's left for his children.

Ness recollects childhood games and flying kites with her father. She tells us he often listened to two pieces of music simultaneously. He started that when we were together, experimenting with my classical albums and his hard rock.

I've stopped concentrating on Ness's words.

Ronan was living with me before he turned eighteen.

He'd left school and started work in the construction industry. There were many well-paid labouring jobs back then. He'd come home sweat-crusted and exhausted. We'd hold each other in the shower, water mixing the heat of our kisses. I'd thought he was happy.

Marco is less articulate. He stumbles over his words, his face puce. There is a distance, as if he hardly knew his father. He talks about heaven, something Ronan didn't believe in.

Someone reads a poem. Ronan couldn't stand poetry.

Svetlana invites people to place flowers on his coffin. Lily-of-the-valley. I wonder where she found them given they're not in season.

The congregation are invited to speak. I rise at the same time as a man in the second pew from the front. He takes to the microphone before I leave my seat, so I sit down again. I don't really have much to say.

I scan the mourners. The likelihood of Kyle being here is remote. Kyle and Ronan were once best friends, but that was a long time ago. My son stopped having anything to do with Ronan at the same time he stopped interacting with me. There's another invitation to speak, but I ignore it as I step out of the church. I pull my collar up against the wind and hesitate for a second. Maybe I should check whether the woman with the hat is actually Jacqui.

But I don't have much to say to her either.

I'm in my Honda looking through my rearview mirror as the bulk of the congregation spill out.

I remember a warm summer night a lifetime ago.

Hungry kisses, lying with an adolescent whose passion shaped the rest of my life.

The rest of my life that is, until now.

Where Your Eyes Used to Be

The first time I took you from your grave, there were spaces where your eyes used to be.

Your taut middle rippled under my fingers, the patterns in your fur familiar, though the bloating was unexpected. I'd thought you might have changed, but had expected a withered carcass, not something turgid.

When I brushed the loam from your body, you felt like an overfull bladder; not the mummified corpse I'd visualised. The skin broke when I rubbed your neck, yielding maggots small as pinpricks.

I returned you to the earth and left you there for a fortnight.

When I did it again, you were wet through, though it hadn't rained. Gritty soil infiltrated your coat. I wanted to shovel earth over your body because you were rank with gases of putrefaction, but I hesitated.

I missed you. I was happy to hold you, despite the odour.

I missed you in many ways. How you'd cry for a feed, then walk around my ankles afterwards, hoping for something better. I missed your old smell, somewhere between stagnant water and sausage fat. I missed your meow, loud and operatic at times, quiet and pitiful at others. I missed you positioning your bottom against my lips, as if doing me a great service.

I put you back.

This morning I took you out again.

You have turned fragile in the last month. My spade almost split you in two. You are dry as sticks, brittle as chalk, your centre hollow. I fold the pieces this way and that. Something scuttles from you into the dirt. It is black and beaded, like an overcooked raisin, but with legs.

You are the colour of soil. Your bones roll like dropped pencils.

I know I have to stop doing this. I have to let you go.

You once inhabited the space between nose and tail, front and backbone.

Now there is nothing but emptiness where your eyes used to be.

When My Uncle
Looks at My Ankles

The skirt feels like animal hide. It's the most appropriate thing I have for Aunt Nona's funeral. My mother bought me this skirt years ago, black gabardine, upholstered in rigid lines around my lower body. I only wear the skirt for formal occasions and court appearances.

My mother is not attending the funeral, though Nona is her only sister. I have come on her behalf. Or that's what I tell anyone who asks. The bristles from my black uniform poke the skin on my legs in silent aggression with a vengeance seldom found in inanimate objects. That is what I have come to expect from this article of shame and sorrow.

My lips fold with mock sincerity around the words of a hymn I've not sung since childhood, and all I can think of is how much I want to shed the skirt and run naked between the aisles shouting hallelujah. The fibres create an illusion of growing out from my body, not in towards me from the skirt. My skin itches as if I have a disease.

When we leave for the reception, Uncle Jonah stares at my chicken-skin ankles. He's only been let out of prison for the day. I know I have committed an offence. It is not seemly to attend one's aunt's funeral with bare-skinned legs, but I can't help it. Since the age of seventeen, I have refused to wear pantyhose. I cannot stand the word, let alone the suffocating grip they confer on my nether-regions. I flick Jonah a sneer, and he looks away, his dimpled chin familiar as childhood.

Cousin Desiree holds her finger to the dimple in her chin, and flits between elderly relatives as if she is offering them the sacrament. A benediction here, a blessing there, receiving kisses from her mother's withered friends and the lipsticked gentry of our wider family. And all the time, my skirt threatens to overwhelm me.

When Constance rang to say her mother had *passed away*, as if she were playing a game of football in a distant town, Mum had feigned a migraine. She refused to speak to her niece. I'd scribbled the funeral date and directions to the crematorium on the back of a takeaway menu. My mother had said, *if you think I'm going to give them the satisfaction,* (snorting like a horse), *you've got another thing going.*

But, I'd countered. *You have to. She's your sister.*

Was, Mum retaliated, a wry smile curving the yellow of her face.

Desiree and Constance could do with the support, I'd said.

Desiree and Constance can go to hell on a number two bus, she'd replied. Mum has always struggled with idioms. *And if you are going yourself,* she'd added, *wear something decent.*

The priest places a sausage roll on his paper plate, and I am filled with sorrow, not for my aunt but for the loss of all things living. I pick the vegetarian option from the platter Constance's husband holds beneath my nose. His eyes linger on my breasts, and then skim to my ankles. I wish I'd shaved my legs this morning.

The last time I'd worn the skirt was in February. I'd appeared in court, eyes lowered, heart racing. Hot as hell, I had sweated under the glare of the magistrate's fury and tied myself in incriminating circles. I'd accepted my sentence and faked contrition. Shoplifting was in my blood, but sometimes blood isn't all it's cracked up to be.

Uncle Jonah catches me when I'm leaving. *Tell your mother I asked after her,* he says with mischief in his eyes. He pats my bottom with his left hand, his right tucked discreetly into its sleeve. He is glued to the prison officer next to him, the handcuffs barely visible. I wish the skirt would bite him and send him to another hell, somewhere he might roast as I did in the courtroom in February. *Go fuck yourself,* I hiss in his ear, loud enough for him and the black-suited officer to hear. No one else does.

The skirt swishes against my legs like a curtain. Sliding into my car, I race back home. My arse is still in a sweat where Jonah smacked me.

Through my tears, I imagine Mum, a teenager in awe of her older sister and the handsome husband. Uncle Jonah was good-looking back then, if the family photos are to be believed. The roguish smile, the presents that fell off the back of a lorry, the toys at Christmas, just for me, always as good as anything Desiree and Constance were given. That Kirk Douglas dimple on his gorgeous chin.

That dimple, just like mine.

The Little Blue Boat

I'm determined to take this holiday despite the uncertainty.

Zeb booked it over a year ago. Things happened: some beyond our control, others hard to control, but under our jurisdiction. Unavoidable events led to cancellations, re-bookings and then further cancellations.

Things changed between us during that time.

Now the itinerary is the same, but the dates are different. The destinations are as planned, but the anticipation and excitement have gone.

"Sure you still want to do this, Otto?" He looks up from folding socks into his case. Sometimes Zeb addresses me by name because he wants to create some distance between us. Because when you've been together as long as we have, why do you need names?

"Why? Don't you?" I won't be pushed into a decision.

We've been hanging together by a thread for months, and I'm not going to be the one who pulls the strands apart to destroy it. If he wants to, then that's his prerogative.

For now, we have things to do.

The dogs need to be settled at the kennels.

We must call Zoë so she knows what to water in the garden, and what's to be left alone. Zeb's sister has a way with plants, and it's not a good one. She kills them. I would have asked his mother. She'd have kept everything alive, especially the roses, but he won't hear of it. Zeb thinks his mother doesn't like him, but he despises her too much to let her in. He has a way of keeping people out.

We've updated the travel insurance, arranged the currency.

He's compiled a list of things we mustn't forget: Insect repellant. Check. Sun cream. Check. Wide-brimmed hat and sunglasses. Check. Driver licence. Check. Waterproof jackets. Check. Medication. Check.

He packs his pills in a separate bag. We used to share a drug box: travel sickness tablets for me, migraine medication for him. Loperamide. Paracetamol.

Zeb throws a novel onto the pile. It's one he started reading months ago that I thought he'd never finish. He adds a crossword book for me. He's never been interested in puzzles. His actions puzzle me at times.

Our city shrinks into the distance as the aircraft gains height. I hate this part of the flight. I'd hold his hand, but I don't want to give him unwanted affection, not while we are trapped in metal. When we reach cruising altitude, I realise I've been clenching my jaw. I would ask him now what he wants; what I can give him, but there's no escape for warring lovers at thirty-three thousand feet. Locked in silence, cursed by inflight entertainment.

A driver intercepts our cases, luggage carts pulled this way and that – our eyes fuzzed with sleep as we are pressed into a different time zone, a parallel world that runs alongside our own. But there is no such thing as our world. Zeb's world is not my world, and my world is a lonely place.

He squeezes lemon over his seafood, breaks crab legs, pulls meat out and sucks the juices. The way his mouth works reminds me of softer times. The camp waiter has placed a single candle on our table. Zeb's tongue piercing flashes bright when he licks his fingers. He has a tiny silver snake in the midline. Now you see it, then you don't. He wipes his lips with a cotton serviette, and I want to cry.

"You okay?" he asks.

"Just tired," I reply. I am tired, but that's not why my eyes are wet.

"It's just that – "

"What?" I shouldn't interrupt him, but I'm not sure I want to hear what comes next.

"Are you sad, Otto?" There it is again. Zeb enunciates my name, as if he is a schoolteacher or a counsellor.

"I'm okay." I squeeze lemon on my prawns. "Glad we're talking about it, though."

"I've been thinking we – "

The camp waiter arrives, singsongs his query about whether the meal is to our satisfaction. The moment dies with our answers.

We've booked a room with twin beds. The travel agent recommended it. Best not to draw attention to our homosexuality in a country such as this, we've been told. From what I've read about the nightlife here, gay relationships may be taboo, but it's not as if that sort of activity is non-existant. He's reading the book. The bedside lamp emits its sickly yellow glow. I could attempt a crossword, but my eyes are closing.

I wonder if he'll go out into the night after I fall asleep? Will he leave me on my own? Will he be safe by himself? Will he be by himself?

I have always loved the roar of the ocean. There is a hole in my shoe. My sock swims in sand. We've walked for an hour or more. There are sea cucumbers and starfish in the water – black as sewer rats and poisonous blue, both with the velveteen skin marine creatures have. I've heard the fish here will bite you, but they won't kill you. It'll take an hour or more to walk back to the hotel. We're not in a hurry. It's not as if we have anywhere else we need to be.

We stop walking and sit on a rocky knoll.

"Do you see that?" he asks.

"What?"

"Over there." He points to the distance, beyond the reef where the waves crash like wrestlers fighting to win.

"What is it?" There's a speck, tossing and twisting. His eyesight has always been better than mine.

"It's a boat. A little blue boat."

I wish I'd brought binoculars.

"Where do you think it will go?" I ask.

"I really don't know," he says. "I wish I did."

He looks at me, and he might be crying, or it could be sea spray on his eyes.

The Suicide
Trading Card Scheme

That summer, there was nothing for me to do with my hands, and even less for me to do with my mind.

The air was dry, and the smell of grass got into everything.

"I'm sending you to Uncle Bram's," Mum said, waving a knife. "You could help on the farm." She cut a radish in half.

"But – "

"You need to do *something*, Nathan," she said. "Can't sit around here like a dead fish." She sliced a carrot. "I'll come over for Christmas."

"What – "

"It'll do you good."

Later, Mum's sugary telephone-voice drifted through.

" ... no Kat, I'm not sending Rache, just Nathan ... school holidays ..."

So I'd be at Willow Haven all summer.

My uncle had a farm near Arthur's Pass. It had to be the loneliest place in New Zealand. Mum told Aunt Kat I'd be useful, like I was a carthorse or dishwasher.

She said nothing about my *accident*.

Mum rarely mentioned the *accident*. S'pose she had lots on her mind, what with Rache's bulimia and her own twisted headspace.

Rache and I had spent many summers at Willow Haven when we were young. Bram and Kat kept several thousand head of Romney sheep.

The sheep were stupid, running from one field to another. Two Border Collies, Blue Martin and Scarlett, rounded them with the efficiency of robots.

Willow Haven was fun as a kid. I'd throw pebbles into the stream, feed sour apples to the horse on the next farm then watch it puke froth.

Working for my uncle was exhausting but paid well. Bram wouldn't want me though if he knew I'd swallowed 110 paracetamol tablets in September. I'd had my stomach pumped and had been in hospital. He'd worry about my sanity.

The overdose was harrowing, but it was no *accident*. I'd known what I was doing.

Mum calling it an *accident* was what Ms. Cooper my English teacher might term a *euphemism*. I can't blame my mother. She'd suffered depression since Dad left. One barmy twin was enough. Rache and I *both* going mental was too much.

Mum had been on anti-depressants for a year but was still as screamy as ever. Withering sighs wafted from the kitchen like steam, like she was willing us to check on her.

Whenever we did, all we got was, "I'm fine." Then she'd go back to peeling, scrubbing or chopping ... and sighing.

I'd tried Mum's Citalopram the first time.

I woke with a tingling in my arm. Probably to do with the position I'd slept in rather than the pills I'd stolen. But I was still very much alive.

The next time, I did more research. Jumping under trains or hanging weren't reliable. Paracetamol wasn't fast, but it was very poisonous if you took enough.

But it hadn't worked. Nothing works if you chicken out. You can't un-jump from a tall building. But if you've taken an overdose, you can walk into the A and E department in a T-shirt polka-dot boxer shorts as I did, shouting, "help me!" and your attempted suicide is all over.

Afterwards, I had counselling and received what Ms. Cooper would have termed *platitudes*. They sent me to group therapy.

That's where I met XXY.

We had to introduce ourselves to the person next to us.

"Who *are* you, anyway?" The gaunt figure pointed at my nametag, "Who is *Nathan*?" The way the creep said *Nathan* made it sound like I had a disease, which I suppose I did. We all did. The moron wanted to know what lay behind my name, but I was too scared to say. So I counter-attacked.

"What, are you like Prince or something?" I prodded the name badge and my finger sank unexpectedly into soft flesh. "Identifiable only by a symbol?"

"Nah, that's my name, *ecs-ecs-why.*"

If anyone had asked me to describe XXY then, I'd have struggled to find the right *pronouns,* as Ms. Cooper called them.

He. She. It.

With slender legs, roundish face and hint of a bust, my new acquaintance seemed both male *and* female. I couldn't flat out ask *hey, are you a dude or a chick*? But XXY didn't keep me guessing for long. With an intense look, this person I'd just met told me about their weird condition — can't remember what it was called.

"But do I say *he* or *she*?" I'd asked.

"Easy." XXY said. "It's like I'm lots of people. They. Their. Them."

XXY was one of the oddest creatures I'd ever seen, though I hadn't seen the bizarre sheep on Bram's farm back then.

XXY wasn't rude, just odd. Like me. We talked for a bit.

"I live quite near here," they said, pulling their hoodie sleeve up to reveal a thin wrist. It wasn't a conscious gesture. The wrist was scarred with a zigzag of cuts. "We could grab a drink."

"Sure," I said.

~

XXY's room was crazy, posters over the walls, the usual sixties rock-gods, but also pictures of galaxies and supernovas and birds in flight. They flicked a switch, and a plasma ball glowed like a tentacled creature. A massive scan of a brain filled the ceiling.

That was when they showed me their collection of trading cards.

"What are they *for*?" I asked.

"It's like a network. We swap them."

"Some of these are gross."

"Yeah. I guess."

I flicked through the box. I must have picked the worst first – a laminated brown smear labelled *Kathleen's shit, 13th February 2016. This is how I feel.* I picked another, thicker, but just as goofy, a realistic looking ear. It was shaped from modelling clay, with red blood and grey gristle at the join, sewn onto the card with a spiderwork of stitches. *Vincent was right,* written in tiny letters beneath.

There were others. Pictures of dead things cut and pasted from magazines. Drawings of huge eyes crying crystals. Deformed genitalia in pastel watercolours.

"I'm not convinced these make me feel better," I said.

"They're not supposed to," XXY said. "They're just supposed to make you *feel*."

I put the box aside, and leafed through their collection of vinyl.

We saw each other often after that, but I didn't join the Suicide Trading Card Scheme.

Not then, anyway.

~

The day I arrived at the farm that summer, everything was a bit off, and that was even before I saw the odd sheep.

Anyone familiar with Romney sheep knows they're big, with dangling drag-queen ears. There are more Romneys than human beings in NZ. The sheep are not known for their grace, more the length of fibre in their fleeces. They make good eating too. With Christmas coming, Bram was selecting lambs for slaughter.

He didn't ask me to do anything on the first day, so I sat around like a dead fish.

He didn't ask me to do much on the second day either.

Or the third.

I went to the local shop on day three. It was thirty minute's walk away. Items were randomly arranged on shelves, no two alike. The shopkeeper looked at me with lowered brows, as if to say, *you don't belong.* She passed me my phone credit and asked if I needed anything else. No smile, no small talk.

I shook my head.

"No soap?" she persisted.

Did I smell?

"What about a paper. I've got yesterday's. You can have it half price." I guess she was desperate. "Postage stamps?"

I hesitated then bought a pack.

At the farm, I loaded the credit and texted XXY. *Okay, I'm in,* I messaged. *How do I join the Scheme?*

I waited for a reply.

~

Aunt Kat cooked hearty meals on an old cast-iron stove the size of a mini-bus. She'd ask me to lay the table, scrub pots and pans, but didn't say much. She was preoccupied with farm business. I'd nicked cigarettes from her handbag before I discovered an easier way to get my smokes. I'd taken her lighter too. Smoking in the apple orchard, I'd stare at the sky.

Bram and Kat's farmhouse was enormous, with several flights of stairs threading through the building like arteries and veins. There were unoccupied rooms leading off various corridors. Rooms waiting to be filled with children my aunt and uncle never had.

At dinner, my uncle filled his plate, and ate like he was still working. He sawed methodically through his bread, chew chew chew swallow, chew chew chew swallow, with military precision.

Uncle Bram was set in his ways. He never cooked. He never wore blue. He smoked in silent desperation, like he needed to fill his inner emptiness with tobacco-fumes. He bulk bought his baccy, and made rollies with his fat fingers.

Bram's tobacco was easy to nick, several pouches open at any time. I never had to hide the smell either, because the cedar-wood scent of rolling-tobacco hung all over the house like a ghost.

The sheep found me smoking in the orchard, joining cloud-shapes in my mind to form devils and genies. The animals liked me, followed me around, looking up with dispirited eyes, until Blue Martin or Scarlett directed them somewhere else.

One lamb with a dark fleck above his eye bleated like a human baby and trotted to me whenever he could.

I named him Patrick.

I'd been picking clusters of wool that had caught in the fencing, collecting it in my pocket. Maybe I could become a sheep farmer. Ms. Cooper had encouraged me to look for a *vocation*. She'd said I should talk to people about work.

On the fourth evening, I lay in the orchard and saw a strange sheep in the distance. It sneered at me, fierce, incomplete in the shadows. There was something missing.

That night, I borrowed Aunt Kat's sewing box, and made my first trading card.

Rache usually saw more of our father than I did. I'd last met him in a café with dull Formica tables. He talked about the loveless marriage he'd had with our mother. Dad reckoned it was the real deal with Miriam though. I think it had more to do with her long legs and flat stomach. Miriam was fresh chicken to my mother's gristly brisket.

Miriam was much younger than Dad. She looked tidy, until you saw her eyes. She had mad eyes and tiny ears that stuck out of her pixie-head like ten-cent-pieces.

I don't know what had got me thinking about Dad. Maybe it was those strange sheep with broad faces, anger in their eyes, and tiny stumps where the ears should have been.

Like ten-cent-pieces.

Mum and Rache arrived at Willow Haven on Christmas morning, my sister's face like pumice, grey and pocked. This time of year was hard for her.

Later I unblocked the sink in the bathroom and tried to piece together parts of her vomit that had once been Patrick.

On Boxing Day, Mum and Rache left early. Bram showed me how to use his hunting rifle. He said there'd been a wild pig lurking beyond the orchard, and he wanted it for New Year's dinner.

"You want a smoke, Nathan?" he asked whilst demonstrating the safety catch.

"No, I don't — "

"Look. You only have to ask. But I'd rather you *did* ask."

I said nothing.

I began running to the shop every day. Six days after I'd sent my first Trading Card, they had an envelope for me. My first attempt had been rough and untidy, a smear of fence-wool sewn onto the card, and a spiral of writing about stomach pumping. I'd called it *Washout*. I was surprised to receive something so soon, what with the holiday post.

I tore into the envelope and found a card covered in violet cloth, a skull stitched onto the fabric. The letters too, had been sewn, not written.

What if our suffering outlives us?

There was a note with their card.

Nathan,

Thank you for Washout.

Kisses, Briar.

Briar. Someone called Briar who knew the kind of pain that filled your muscles, joints and bones, pain that sat behind your eyes and decayed your brain. Someone who wondered if despair stayed in your empty shell after you had gone.

Shit.

The rules were that I had to send my next card to someone different, not Briar. As I ran towards Willow Haven, I thought about my latest card, messy and ragged compared to Briar's. I was useless at drawing or sewing, but had shaped wool into an outline of a sheep's head, held it in place using needle and thread. Couch stitch, Aunt Kat called it.

I almost ran into Bram at the farm, a pig carcass hung over his shoulder like a sack. The last light of life shone in the creature's eyes, an accusation in its hollow glare. My uncle and I nodded to each other, but nothing was said.

Another deformed sheep crept behind him on the hill then disappeared.

I climbed up to my room, breathless, and almost pissed myself with shock. Someone was sitting on my bed.

"Jeez Ecs, you scared the shit out of me."

They turned and nodded. "Hey, Nathan."

"How did you get in? Does Aunt Kat know you're here?"

"I have my ways," XXY said. Looking at my trading card in its unfinished state, they turned it in their fingers. "Not bad."

The sheep on my card had no horns. Romneys don't.

And the sheep had no ears.

I didn't know how to draw ears. It looked *ominous*. That's the word Ms. Cooper would have used. Ominous, with its huge button eyes. Ominous words underneath.

To live to be eaten.

"I got my first card!" Briar's card slipped from my fingers into XXY's, and I tried hard to suppress an exploding smile.

"Not bad," they said again, and tossed it onto my bed.

I'd nicked a cigar from Bram's box. I struggled to ignite it with Kat's lighter. We smoked it together, passing it like a joint.

Someone set a fire in the barn.

If Blue Martin hadn't barked like a lunatic, Bram and Kat would have lost a lot more than they did. The police arrived just after dawn, along with a dude from the fire service. Grey pools of water formed in the mud beneath charred beams. The guy reckoned the fire had been lit on purpose. I don't know how he knew. I watched him poke probes into stuff, noticed him looking at me cautiously, lids lowered.

The guy watched me watching him until Kat called me in for dinner.

Remembering what Ms. Cooper had said about vocations, I looked *fire service* up on the Internet. You didn't need N.C.E.A. or any exams, just had to sit something called a cognitive ability test and have a load of physical checks. I reckon I could do it. I was strong. Real strong. Dad had told me I was *crazy strong* for my age last time we'd had a tussle.

XXY and I slept head-to-toe on my bed.

The next morning, I ran to the shop and posted my sheep trading card to some dude called Richard. His picture on the website was awful. Hollow dweeb-eyes.

He deserved *To live to be eaten.*

As I ran back towards Willow Haven, I noticed two sheep silhouetted in hazy sunlight. When they turned, I saw they didn't have ears. I tripped and nearly fell. When I looked up again the sheep were gone.

Back in the farmhouse, my heart thumped in my chest.

Aunt Kat asked why I hadn't phoned my mother.

"She's been asking for you, Nathan. Rache is in hospital again." My aunt's voice cracked. "She's sick."

I didn't call my mother.

My heart thumped in my chest.

My heart thumped in my chest.

Blue Martin died. Uncle Bram thought he'd been poisoned. I don't know how he knew. Perhaps it was the pool of blood stained vomit next to his body.

There are lots of things on a farm that can poison a dog.

I used a snippet of the dog's fur on my third trading card.

XXY slept in my bed again that night, but not head-to-toe.

My heart thumped in my chest.

~

It was dark. XXY must have followed me outside. Their hand came down on my shoulder.

My heart thumped in my chest.

"What are you doing out here?" I hissed, Uncle Bram's rifle in my hands.

"I could ask you the same," XXY said. "Come inside, Nathan. Put the gun away."

"But I'm so close," I said, "so very close."

"Close to what?"

"Knowing."

My heart thumped in my chest.

"Those sheep. They know."

My heart thumped in my chest.

"Come inside."

"They're laughing at me."

"Leave it, Nathan."

"They're laughing at us, at how humans have got everything wrong. So wrong."

~

Aunt Kat never used to say that much to me. Now she says nothing.

I haven't called my mother. Rache could be dead, and I wouldn't know. But at last I understand why she can't keep her food down.

My heart thumps in my chest.

Uncle Bram's not looking so good. Scarlett sits a silent vigil by his feet.

Every day she sits a little further away.

~

It's awful quiet at Willow Haven.

I toy with the rifle in my hands.

The mutant sheep are everywhere, tiny flaps where their ears should be.

The sirens draw me to the window.

My heart thumps in my chest.

Three police vans screech to a halt in front of the farmhouse. For a second I think my vocation might be with the armed offenders squad, but the thought passes quickly.

The oak door creaks as it is kicked in.

My heart thumps in my chest.

They lock my arm behind me and push me to the ground.

I scream. My shoulder hurts. I tell them about the sheep. XXY can vouch for me, I tell them. They have to find XXY, I shout.

But as I say it, I know they won't.

They never can.

I'm in this on my own.

As I always have been.

The Baby

The child doesn't look like anyone in our family. At a push, you could say he has his great-grandfather's forehead. He seems darker than Abe, though it's hard to tell so soon. He could still be reddened from the birth. The baby might take after Brenda, but I know very little about our son's partner. I know even less about the man who fathered my granddaughter's child.

I don't see anything of myself in the baby, but he's a part of me. I will keep him safe.

Last month, Abe phoned, asked if we could meet for coffee.

"Sure," I said. I had a full work schedule, but I always made time to see my ex-husband. It was the only way to discover how our son and his family were. Kyle hadn't spoken to me for years. "Can you make Thursday?" I asked. "I finish work at six."

"Not sure what'll be open then," Abe said. There was a muffled conversation. "Sondrine's suggesting dinner here. We need to talk to you about something."

I didn't ask what the *something* was. "Don't want to put you to any trouble." I'd rather have met on neutral ground. Abe's wife's *niceness* has always been difficult for me.

He put Sondrine on. "It's no trouble, Madeleine. I'll make boeuf bourguignon." She may have been infuriatingly perfect, but Sondrine's boeuf bourguignon was to die for.

On Thursday, I took honey and ginger sponge with a matched dessert wine. The meat was tender, the wine well chosen and the conversation lively. If there was *something* important they needed to discuss, neither mentioned it.

I served dessert and forced the issue.

"How's Kyle?" Whatever it was had to involve our son.

I hadn't spoken to Kyle since he was seventeen. Abe and Sondrine had helped over the years. They kept me updated, showed me photographs of my son and the grandchildren. They were supportive when Kyle rejected my attempts to reconnect. They'd wanted to invite me over when the grandchildren were staying with them, but Kyle had vetoed the idea. Those kids had little to do with me, but I wanted a connection.

"There *is* something," Abe said.

"Is Kyle all right?" I asked. "What about Cam and Eva? Brenda?"

"They're fine." Abe cleared his throat. "Well, not really."

"It's Eva," Sondrine said.

"What's happened?" The granddaughter I'd never met was nearly fifteen.

"She's pregnant," Abe said.

I didn't know what to say.

"The whole thing came to a head a few weeks ago," Sondrine added. "No one knew. She'd concealed it."

"Is she all right?" I wanted to know who'd done that to Eva. I wanted to kill him.

"The father's an older man," Abe said, as if he'd read my thoughts. "Married."

A child seduced by someone who should know better. Kyle's words from years ago echoed in my mind.

This is fucked up, Mum.

How could you?

There's a word for people like you.

"Has he been reported?"

Fucking hypocrite. Hadn't I done the same thing? Didn't I destroy my relationship with my son when I seduced his best friend? But what I'd had with Ronan was different, wasn't it? I'd loved him. He'd loved me. Hadn't he?

"She won't name him." Sondrine placed her hand on my shoulder. "Madeleine, are you all right?" I was shaking. The woozy-headed post-wine glow had gone, but I felt a different kind of dizziness.

"I'm fine." I lied. "But she's so young."

"She needs help," Sondrine said. "At least until the baby is born."

"Kyle can't handle it," Abe said. "He won't talk to her."

I wanted to shake my son. Yet hadn't I helped make him into what he was?

"Who's supporting her?" I asked.

They told me the authorities were involved. A social worker had been appointed.

"Kyle and Brenda haven't gone as far as throwing Eva out," Sondrine said, "but things are difficult. She feels they're judging her."

"She says she can't stay with them." Abe frowned, and dragged his fork through the mess that remained on his plate.

"For Kyle," Sondrine added, "it's about shame. That's a big thing for him. Eva made a mistake. She knows that. But she wants the best for her baby."

"We've asked her to move in with us," Abe said. "At least until the birth."

"Can I help at all?"

I wanted to protect the young woman and her unformed child that was part of me.

I asked more questions. They filled me in.

Abe drove south to collect Eva. Sondrine asked me over to their house, and we prepared a room for Eva and the baby. We busied ourselves clearing drawers, putting fresh linen on the bed. I placed the crib I'd bought in the corner.

We opened the door to greet her when she arrived.

Eva was tentative, fragile. Although she looked familiar from the photos and movie clips I'd seen, when you hear someone speak in person, it's different.

She let me hold her. I could feel the bones of Eva's shoulders when I hugged her. I didn't want to let her go.

Something passed between us. There are times you don't need words. She knew about me. She knew why her father had kept me away from her and her brother. That knowledge turned me into an ally.

Eva and I are still getting to know each other. I go over whenever I can, between my shifts, and when I sense she needs me most.

Sondrine rang this morning. It was time. I met them at the hospital.

We take turns to sit with Eva as the contractions come faster and harder. But it is me she asks for at the final hurdle.

It is me she hands the slippery baby to soon after he is born.

We understand each other.

We will love this child.

Previously Published

- 'Seven Lesbians and a Bar of Soap', *runner up Alternative Bindings Wallace Arts Prize,* 2016.
- 'The Carpet', *Firefly,* 2015.
- 'Appetite', *Degenerate Literature,* 2016.
- 'The Night My Sister Leaves', *Blue Fifth Review,* 2017.
- 'Balloon Phobia and God', *Alluvia,* 2017.
- 'Bagdogra Airport', *We are a Website,* 2017.
- 'The Size of the Lie', *Fictive Dream,* 2017.
- 'Where Your Eyes Used To Be', *New Flash Fiction Review,* 2018.
- 'When My Uncle Looks At My Ankles', *Fictive Dream,* 2019.
- 'The Suicide Trading Card Scheme', *Takahē,* 2017.

Thanks

Eileen Merriman, who provided valuable critique for many of these stories.

Matt Potter, for his trust and belief, and for inventing the *Lifespan* series that provided the basis for the Madeleine and Ronan stories.

John XY, for the source material that provided inspiration for the Zeb and Otto stories.

Also from Truth Serum Press

truthserumpress.net/catalogue/

- *Where the Wind Blows* by Sandra Arnold
  978-1-923000-22-3 (paperback) 978-1-923000-26-1 (ePub)
- *Hold Off the Night* by Teresa Burns Gunther
  978-1-922427-00-7 (paperback) 978-1-922427-18-2 (ePub)
- *Remembering the Dead* by Lewis Woolston
  978-1-922427-58-8 (paperback) 978-1-922427-62-5 (ePub)

- *How to Catch Flathead* by Peter Michal
  978-1-925536-94-2 (paperback) 978-1-925536-95-9 (ePub)
- *Easy Money* by Steve Evans
  978-1-925536-81-2 (paperback) 978-1-925536-82-9 (ePub)
- *The Last Free Man* by Lewis Woolston
  978-1-925536-88-1 (paperback) 978-1-925536-89-8 (ePub)

www.ingramcontent.com/pod-product-compliance
Lightning Source LLC
Chambersburg PA
CBHW021220260626
47172CB00002B/523